DARK PATH OF DESIRE

Herbert Grosshans

DARK PATH OF DESIRE

DOUBLE DRAGON

Chapter One

Claire Belmont sat on one of the lounges on the patio behind her ten-million-dollar mansion and stared into the clear water of her heated pool. She felt restless, fidgety, and alone.

Allan, her husband, was out playing golf or doing who-knows-what with his buddies and probably wouldn't be home for a couple of days. He did that a lot these days.

After his brother's death, things changed between her and Allan. He used to be an attentive husband, but now he seemed cold and distant most of the time. They hadn't had sex since the accident that took Andy's life. He even blamed her for enticing Andy to go riding with her. Andy had loved horses and riding. Liz, his wife, did not share his passion, but Claire did. When Andy asked her to go riding with him, she accepted. They spent many afternoons riding their horses.

On the day of the accident, Claire challenged Andy to a race. During the race, their horses collided and Andy was thrown. He broke his neck and died on the scene.

Liz accused her of having had an affair with Andy. Something that wasn't true. They had been good friends, nothing more.

She didn't blame Allan for mourning his brother's death. Losing a family member is always a terribly tragedy. It must be worse when it's your twin. She missed Andy, too. He had been a fun-loving guy, always telling jokes, always in a good mood, the way Allan used to be.

How long does one mourn? Is two years too long or not enough? She was thirty and not getting any younger. Her sexual appetite had always been great. She needed to lie in the strong arms of a man and feel the touch of his hands on her breasts, on her belly and shudder beneath him as he gently caressed her pussy. There was no greater pleasure than the moment when he spread her thighs with his hand and guided his hard penis into her. Nothing could match the ecstasy she experienced when his manhood exploded inside her clutching pussy as she milked him until he was dry and limp.

A soft sigh escaped her lips as she fantasized about it. It wasn't only the sex she missed. She longed to be held, to be cuddled, to hear the loving words of a lover, to be kissed and to feel safe in his arms, to feel the gentle touch of his hand on her cheek. She didn't remember the last time she shared a bottle of wine in an intimate setting with a man that loved her, or when she took a walk under the stars on a warm summer evening, his arm around her waist.

She was ripped out of her dark mood when the phone rang. It was her friend Carmen Garcia. "Hey Claire, do you feel like driving down to the ranch? Randy called. The horses are getting restless and need to be taken out for a ride. It's a beautiful day, and there is nothing more exhilarating than sitting bare-assed on the back of a horse with your hair flying in the wind as you gallop down a lonely mountain trail."

Claire chuckled softly. "Bare-assed, huh? First of all, that must be mostly uncomfortable and secondly, one of these days you'll find your picture

6

on some website featuring your bare ass among all those other nude girls."

"Now who would take that picture? Come on, girlfriend, don't be a spoilsport."

"I'm never a spoilsport and you know it. Right now, I'm not in the mood for doing anything, but maybe it would do me good to get out a little. I feel as restless as the horses."

"So, what are you waiting for? I'll pick you up in forty minutes. Be ready."

One thing with Carmen, when she said forty minutes, she'd be there. She didn't disappoint this time, either. She pulled up in her convertible exactly forty minutes from the time she got off the phone.

Claire was ready. Dressed in her riding outfit, she sat on one of the planters edging her circular driveway.

As usual, Carmen's long black hair hung unruly past her shoulders. Claire knew it covered the tattoo of a roaring lion in her neck. When Claire asked her once why a lion, Carmen had just smiled and said, "Why not?"

The lion may not be visible, but Carmen's naked arms exhibited her other tattoos, as did the generous exposed part of her ample breasts. Claire could never understand why anyone as beautiful as Carmen would do that to herself and ruin her soft brown skin forever.

When not tanned, Claire's skin was white and without a blemish. It was no accident. She took good care of her skin and body, spending thousands of dollars on beauty products and services. No tattoo on her arms or anywhere else on her body would ever destroy their nearly flawless condition.

Or maybe just a small butterfly in the small of her back. She could see herself getting one of those, but so far had never taken the step to do it. She had to admit, she was scared of needles.

Contrary to Carmen, Claire didn't like to get her hair messed up. She knew Carmen would be driving with the top of her convertible down, so she had taken precautions and hid her blond hair under a baseball cap.

"Are you just going to sit there or are you coming?" Carmen called to her, beckoning with one hand.

"What's the rush? The horses aren't going anywhere." She got up from her spot and walked to the car. Getting into the seat, she sighed.

"You seem so down. What's the problem?"

"I'm bored."

Carmen threw her a sidelong glance as she pulled out of the driveway. "That's why I'm here to keep you busy and entertained."

"And I appreciate it." She put a hand on Camilla's arm. "I'm grateful and lucky to have you as a friend."

"I'm always there for you, but you know that."

"I know, but I need more than just a good friend. I need the love of a man."

"In other words, you're horny. Well, then there should be no problem." Camilla laughed. "Randy was wondering if you'd come along. I told him you would."

"Randy is just a diversion. Somebody to scratch an itch. I need more than that."

"What's the story with you and Allan anyway? Has anything changed between you two? I still

8

remember when you told me he was the man of your dreams and you'd always be in love."

"That was four years ago. He was a different man then. The day Andy died, something died in Allan also. Sometimes I have the feeling he hates me."

"Do you still love him?"

Claire shook her head. "How can you love a man who barely looks at you? To him I'm a ghost who shares the same house with him. We hardly talk and don't sleep together anymore. At least, he gave me the master bedroom. He sleeps in the guestroom."

"So why don't you divorce him? You're a beautiful woman, still young enough to find another man. I can recommend a good lawyer. He'll make you a rich woman when you divorce Allan."

"No, I won't be rich. When we got married, Allan made me sign a prenuptial agreement, stating if I should ever leave him for any reason, I wouldn't get a dime. He said he felt guilty for doing that, but his lawyer had insisted on it."

"That sucks. How about if Allan divorces you? Or did you sign that away also?"

"Allan will never give me a divorce. He's a good Catholic, you know."

"Even good Catholics get divorced if they have a good reason. You'll have to give him one. If you can get him to divorce you, we've got him by the balls. My lawyer will take him to the cleaners." Camilla laughed merrily as if she had just told a joke.

'What do you suggest I do?"

"That's easy. Fuck every guy that wants you."
She laughed again. "If it gets known you're
available, they'll be breaking down your door with
their dick in hand."

"You're so crude." Claire smiled. "Your idea
sounds great, but I don't believe Allan cares enough
at this stage if I cheat on him or not."

"It'll be worth a try. If nothing else, you won't
be bored anymore, or lonely. And you'll have fun
doing it."

"I don't know. I'm not a prostitute."

"You won't be, because you don't charge for it.
That's the beauty of it. You won't be breaking any
laws. This is a free country, Sweetheart. No woman
has ever been charged for fucking a man for free."
She chuckled. "If you have doubts and want to
protect yourself even more, my lawyer can hook
you up with a judge. Once you fuck him, he'll be
putty in your hands."

"Somehow that doesn't feel right."

"Why not? You're not a blushing young virgin
anymore. I know you love sex. How old were you
when you lost your virginity?"

"I was thirteen. It was with a boy who lived a
few houses down from mine. We only did it once,
but it awoke inside me a craving I needed to still. I
was well developed for my age and finding willing
older boys was easy, and they believed me when I
told them I was sixteen."

Carmen snickered. "I was the same age as you
when it happened to me. Only the guy who
introduced me to sex was thirty years old. You ever
done it with a mature man when you were that
tender age?"

10

"I found other girls, slightly older than me, who were also already into sex. We formed a secret ring and started having sex with older men. For money, of course. We used to hang out at the golf course where all the horny old geezers played golf, trying to get away from their wives. 'My wife's all dried up,' more than one told me. 'I still have lots of juice left in me'. And they usually did." She smiled, thinking about good old Steffan and the others. Most of them were probably dead now.

"At sixteen, I became a cheerleader with the Rocktown Rockets and it was even easier then to find horny old men." She laughed. "Sometimes I screwed two guys in a row. I was insatiable. Did I ever tell you I was engaged for about three years?"

Carmen seemed surprised. "Nope. This is news to me."

"Well, I was. He was the captain of the Rocktown Rockets and as handsome as they come. I was nineteen when we got engaged. At twenty-one, I moved in with him. My parents didn't approve, but I was old enough. They did accept it reluctantly, assuming Roy and I would get married anyway. It was a wonderful time in my life. I left him and all that a year later."

"Why?"

"I don't know. Somehow, I felt I needed more. Besides, I needed to get away. Too many men recognized me."

"You said you're not a prostitute. Didn't you ever think you were one when you and your friends screwed all those old men? You did charge for it."

"We did, but none of us saw anything wrong with what we were doing, and we were delighted to earn our own money in such an easy and pleasurable way. It allowed us to buy stuff, but that's all behind me. I'm not proud of that part in my life."

"That's okay. I'm not judging. However, you shouldn't have a problem doing it again. If you follow my advice things will work out."

"How do you know all this?"

"How do you think I got my money? After three husbands I'm an authority."

"You only went through two divorces. Your last husband, Frank, died while you were still married. He's the one who left you all that money."

"That's true, but John and Frederick, my first husbands, paid me a bundle. I had enough to last me for the rest of my life already then. Frank was just the icing on the cake." She heaved a little sigh. "Poor Frank. Rest his soul. He was the best of them all. I really loved him, even though he was old. He always told me I was oversexed and one day I would kill him with my passion. He was right." She sniffed. "His heart gave out, but he died happy."

"I won't be so lucky. Allan is only thirty and as healthy as a horse. Besides, the whole idea won't work. If I cheat on Allan and he finds out, he doesn't have to divorce me, he can kick me out onto the street, without ever paying me a dime. I'll be homeless with no income. I can't marry another man, because I'm still married. And I really don't feel like making a living as a prostitute."

"You won't have to. I'll let you in on a little secret, girlfriend. A woman's pussy is the greatest weapon ever created. Even the most powerful men will surrender to the sight and temptation of a

12

pussy. With that thing between your legs, you can control any man to do your bidding."

Claire sighed. "Not Allan."

"How about Allan's father? Is there any way you can lure him into your bed? He's a man and not immune to the pleasures of the flesh. Let him see you naked. Pretend you're drunk and sit in his lap. Give him a good view of your pussy and your tits and ass. Give him a lap dance if you must. He won't be able to resist the siren call. Let him fuck you more than once. If you can manage that, you'll have him eating out of your hand." She giggled. "Your hand or anything else, if you know what I mean. Don't give up. An opportunity will come along. You just have to recognize it and you will if you pay attention." She let go of the wheel and lifted both hands into the air. "Life is beautiful. All you need to do is live it. And live it you will. We'll make the best of today and enjoy every moment. Forget about Allan and let destiny take you by the hand."

Claire laughed. "Better take the wheel into your hands or neither of us will live past today, my philosopher friend. I think you're a little crazy, but I love you, anyway."

* * *

When they arrived at the ranch, the horses were already saddled and ready to go. The ranch belonged to Joseph Forrest, an old friend of Camilla's late husband.

Joseph Forrest didn't live at the ranch anymore. His son, Randy, looked after the ranch now. Randy

13

was thirty-five, but with his open smile and athletic looks appeared to be twenty-five. He winked at Claire as he helped her onto her horse. Even though she didn't need any help, she let him. "Will you be hanging around a bit after the ride?"

She gave him a teasing smile. "Maybe."

Claire could never figure out why he was still single, but she was positive he was screwing a number of the women and young girls he gave riding lessons, even though he denied it when she brought it up.

She patted the horse's neck when it lifted its head and snorted. It was eager and ready to get going. Taking off her baseball cap, she handed it to Randy and shook her long hair free, letting it cascade down her shoulders.

"I'll race you to the first bluff," Carmen called and took off.

"See you later." Claire blew Randy a kiss and raced after Carmen. She gave the horse free reign, relishing the feeling of freedom as the cool wind caressed her face. For a short moment she forgot all about Allan and the bored life she led.

Carmen beat her to the bluff and waited for Claire to catch up. "For a racehorse Black Lightning is pretty slow," Carmen teased her.

As if understanding what Carmen said, the horse neighed and moved sideways. Claire pulled on the reigns to keep it steady and from bolting away. "Easy, boy," she said with a soothing voice and put her hand on the muscular neck.

"He's as high-strung and restless as his owner," Carmen commented. "Horses are sensitive and react to the mood of its rider. You'd better relax, girl."

"I'm fine." Claire ran her fingers through her hair, but it was already messed up from the wind. "Are you going to take off your clothes now?" She laughed and opened the top of her blouse.

"What?" Carmen gave her a questioning look.

"You said you wanted to ride bare-assed down a lonely mountain trail."

"You didn't take that literally, did you now?"

Claire grinned. "With you I never know. You're as unpredictable as the weather in April."

"That's why I lead such an exciting life. To answer your question—not today but who knows? Maybe the next time." She laughed and turned her horse to face the trail that led into the forest. "Let's go."

The trail was narrow but wide enough for them to ride side-by-side. It wound itself through the forest for a while and then it opened into another valley. There was a lake about a mile away, surrounded by tall trees. Behind the lake, a mountain rose into the sky. Part of the mountain was covered with pine trees, but the top was bare rock. In the wintertime, snow covered the top and the trees. She knew there was a ski lift on the other side, but this side was still unspoiled wilderness.

"I want to stop for a moment and enjoy the view," Claire said. "This must be the most beautiful spot on Earth. I wish it were this beautiful everywhere."

"And as empty of people," Carmen added. "Have you ever imagined how it would be if you were the only woman left on Earth?"

"You mean me and the last man?"

15

"Oh no. Where would the fun be? There'd be lots of men. All of them doing your bidding. You'd be their queen. Just think, a different man every night."

"I'd be their whore. No thank you." Claire shook herself. "With my luck, it would be just me and Allan, anyway."

Carmen made a face. "You're no fun. Now you spoiled my fantasy. Come, let's get down to the lake and go for a swim."

Claire chuckled. "I knew you'd get us naked at some point."

Smirking, Carmen took off down the slight slope toward the lake, but she didn't take the trail. Instead, she chose to ride across the grass-covered meadow. The grass was high, and they rode slow, which suited Claire just fine. It gave her a chance to enjoy the fresh air and the many wild flowers growing among the grass.

Carmen headed for an open spot among the trees. The clearing was not large and offered them protection from being seen by anyone else who might visit the lake. There was a small, sandy beach, and the blue water of the lake was calm.

Carmen jumped off her horse, but Claire sat for a moment and took in the scenery. "This is so beautiful," she exclaimed. "Thanks for getting me out of the house." She had been here many times before, but every time she came to this spot, she admired the tranquil beauty. "You know, I could be happy living here. Just imagine a beautiful cottage right here and seeing this every day."

"Oh, I can imagine it, but I wouldn't want to be alone. Since you're already fantasizing, why not

16

also dream about a handsome hunk of a man who loves you more than anything in the world, and his only goal is to make you happy."

Claire looked up at the sky and nodded. "Yes, that would be wonderful." She sighed. "But that's only a fantasy. I probably would be stuck with Allan."

"Forget about Allan. He seems to consume your every thought and moment. He isn't worth it, girl. Now, come down from that horse, get undressed, and let's go for a swim. The water is calm and probably as warm as a tub."

"That's what you said the last time. I nearly got a heart attack when I jumped into the water." Claire laughed, climbed out of the saddle and slid to the ground. "We'd better tie the horses to a tree. I don't want them to run away."

As she led her horse to a nearby tree, she thought she heard voices. "Did you hear that?"

"What?"

"Voices. Listen."

Listening for a moment, she heard it again. It was definitely a man's voice. "Hear it?"

"Yes, I did. Sounds like some guys arguing."

Claire frowned. "I thought nobody else knew about this lake. There goes my dream."

"It seems to come from that direction." Carmen pointed to their left. "Let's go investigate. Maybe we can pick up a couple of hot guys."

"I'm not so sure. They may not be in the mood."

Carmen laughed. "Maybe we should get naked. That will put them into the mood."

"Don't be silly. Sometimes you act and talk like a sex-starved teenager."

Wiggling her hips, Carmen said, "I may not be a teenager, but I am sex-starved. Come on, let's investigate and find out who is disturbing our serene afternoon."

Carefully, they made their way through the trees. The voices were getting louder. Claire could make out at least two distinct voices, and they were definitely male. "I warned you the last time," one voice shouted.

The other man replied, but she couldn't make out all the words. His voice sounded hysterical and Claire wasn't quite certain if what she heard was correct. "I told you I had no choice…come on…you can't do that…no…" The rest ended abruptly.

"Hold the bastard down," shouted another voice. At least that's what it sounded like to Claire, but she wasn't sure.

Carmen looked at Claire. "Something is happening there. Maybe we should forget about going to find out what it is. I don't like family quarrels."

"I need to know," Claire insisted.

They came to the edge of the woods. There was a car parked in the clearing but nobody was there. She heard splashing sounds, and then somebody said with a subdued voice, "He's taking a long time."

The voice came from the edge of the water, which was hidden from view by a row of shrubs. They crept closer. Crouching, they peered over the shrubs.

18

Claire put her hand over her mouth to stifle a scream. Two men were almost up to their knees in the water. They stood bent over; between them lay a body, half-submerged.

"It looks like somebody drowned," Carmen whispered.

"They drowned him," Claire said fiercely.

"Don't jump to conclusions."

"Didn't you hear them talking?"

"I did, but it sounded garbled. You know, the wind and the forest can make you imagine things that aren't there." She stood up. "Looks to me those guys don't know what to do. I know some first aid." With that she walked around the bushes and headed toward the water.

One of the men looked up. His skin appeared dark behind his beard. He poked the other man and whispered something.

"Do you people need help?" Carmen stepped into the water. "What happened?"

"Joe here stumbled, hit his head on a rock and fell into the water." The man looked at his companion. "Right, Ron?"

"That's right. He knocked himself right out." The other man turned his head. He sprouted a goatee and a thick mustache. "I don't think there's anything you can do, lady. He's gone. Drowned. We'll handle it."

"I know CPR. I used to be a nurse." Carmen sounded urgent. "If you want to help your friend then we shouldn't waste time."

"He isn't our friend," the dark-skinned man said. He smirked. "Just some low-life we did some business with." He ran his hand across his black

19

hair and rubbed his beard. "No need for you to be concerned. Like Ron said, we can handle it."

Claire still stood behind the shrubs. She wanted to yell, "Come back Carmen. Leave it alone. These guys are trouble," but she said nothing, just stood and studied the men, trying to put their appearance into her memory. She didn't know why. She'd be smart to forget the whole thing. Unfortunately, that wasn't the way she handled situation like this. She was too curious and stubborn to let it go.

The guy named Ron looked in her direction and noticed her. "Hey, how many of you are there?" he called. "How long have you been watching us and what do you think you saw?"

"There's only the two of us," Carmen answered before Claire could respond. "We just got here and saw the three of you in the water. I came down as quickly as I could, hoping I could help."

Ron turned back to her. "Well, you can't. I suggest you two curious ladies leave and let us take care of this. Okay?"

"You heard the man," Claire called to Carmen. "Let's go."

"What's your name, Babe?" The bearded guy let his gaze roam over Carmen's curvy body. Claire thought she detected a middle-eastern accent but wasn't quite sure. Somehow, she had an instant dislike for him. He looked handsome with his brown eyes and beard, but she never liked men with a mustache and beard. It looked so—un-American.

Carmen flashed her dark eyes at him. "It's not 'Babe', that's for sure. Nobody talks like that anymore. What country and what century do you come from?"

"What makes you think I'm from another country?"

"It's your accent. I have an ear for it."

"I'm as American as you," he said, a little too loud. "But that has nothing to do with this situation. So, if you don't mind, we'd like to get this guy out of the water and take him to the nearest police station. Just so you know, Ron here is a cop and knows what to do. We have it under control." He reached down to grab one arm of the man in the water, while Ron took the other one. Together, they dragged the limp body toward shore.

"Come on, Carmen," Claire shouted. "I want to go."

"Okay, okay, I'm coming." She waded out of the water and came back to Claire. "Something isn't right," she said with a low voice.

"I know. Another reason to leave." Claire watched the two men open the trunk of their car and shove the dead man's body into it. She had a sudden urge to run as fast and as far away as she could.

"I never did get the dark-skinned guy's name," Carmen said. "He's handsome."

"I don't like him and I don't believe you can actually think like that about him. For all we know, he's a murderer."

"That's only your assumption, Claire. You know what they say: Appearances can be deceiving. Didn't you hear him say his buddy Ron is a cop?"

"I heard, but is it true? You don't know."

Carmen gave her a look of disproval. "Don't always be so suspicious, girl. Sometimes, you have to see the good in people."

"I'm trying to, but I've been disappointed and burned too many times. The last man I trusted was my husband and look what happened." In a sudden fit of anger, she broke off a branch from one of the shrubs that blocked her way on the trail. "I was looking forward to a nice relaxing afternoon," she said fiercely. "Now it has been spoiled."

"The day isn't over yet," Carmen said soothingly. "We still go for that swim. In the nude, if we feel like it." She laughed. "Come on, cheer up. The sun is still shining and the water will still be warm. Not all is lost."

Chapter Two

Claire's dark mood still hadn't lifted when they got back to the ranch. She kept seeing the man lying face-down in the water between the other two men.

Randy greeted them with a big smile. "Did you go swimming?"

"We did." Claire got off the horse.

"Was the water cold? You don't look happy."

"We ran across some guys that just murdered another guy," she said.

"Are you kidding?" Randy gave her an inquiring look. Then he looked at Carmen. "She's kidding, isn't she?"

"She isn't, but if you know Claire, she tends to overdramatize things and assume the worst. Yes, we saw three guys in the water. One was dead. Apparently, he drowned. All by himself. At least, that's what the other two told us. One guy was a cop, so they said."

"Did they drive a yellow sports car?"

Claire looked at him sharply. "How do you know?"

"They drove by here a while ago. That's Ron Salsky. He actually is a cop. There was another guy with him. Dark-skinned, curly, black hair, and a beard."

"You know them?"

"Just Ron, the one with the goatee. He comes by once-in-awhile. He's alright. I didn't see anybody else with them."

"There was. His name is Joe and he was in the trunk," Claire said. "Dead."

"I didn't look in the trunk." He shrugged. "If there was a dead body in the trunk and Ron said the guy drowned then it is so. He's a cop. He wouldn't lie."

"Unless he murdered the guy, then he would," Claire said stubbornly.

"I believe you need some pampering. Why don't you go into the house and freshen up. You know where everything is." He looked at Carmen. "David is coming over in a little while. I told him you'd be here, and he's looking forward to see you again. I'll put some steaks on the barbeque. We'll have a few beers and a good time. What do you say?"

"I'm all for it." Carmen chuckled. "I could use a good time right now. David's a fun-guy and knows how to entertain a girl."

Randy laughed. "He sure does. You girls just go ahead. I'll take the horses to the stable and have Larry rub them down and feed them. See you in a bit."

Carmen and Claire headed for the house. Randy lived alone now. His parents had moved out a couple of years back into a condominium in the city. Randy had a housekeeper who did the cooking and cleaning. She didn't live in the house but in a small guest house in the back of the property. Her sons, Larry and Billy, took care of the horses and helped Randy with other chores.

"Have you ever met Regina?" Carmen asked as they climbed up the wide staircase.

"Randy's sister?"

24

"Yes. Have you met her?"

"I have, but I don't really know her that well. She's quite tall and beautiful. Not married. I think she's a lesbian, but I'm not sure."

"I'm surprised she's not living here. I mean, this is a huge house. Three stories high with so many rooms one can get lost."

"She's moved to the city. Apparently, she was never interested in horses."

They walked into the vestibule and Claire stopped for a moment. It didn't matter how many times she came into this house, she always wondered how they replaced the lightbulbs in the huge chandelier hanging from the high ceiling. This house was so different from the mansion she lived in. Her house was fairly new and modern, while Randy's was a colonial style home. It had undergone many changes since it was built over a hundred years ago.

"Do you believe in ghosts?"

Carmen gave her an astonished look. "Why do you ask? Have you seen one?"

"No, I haven't, but old houses certainly would make good homes for ghosts, don't you think so?"

"I never gave it a second thought. Come one, let's look for the bathroom. I need to put on some make-up." Carmen began climbing the stairs to the second floor where the bathroom was located.

Claire followed her slowly. Her thoughts kept going back to the scene down by the lake. She just couldn't shake it.

When they came out of the bathroom, they heard voices coming from downstairs. Walking into the large living room, Claire saw a couple of men

25

talking to Randy, while two women sat on the couch, holding glasses in their hands.

She had met one of the women before. Her name was Linda Bowman. Tall and slim, dark-haired with smoldering eyes, she looked like a model, which was befitting for the head of a modeling agency.

Claire also knew the man she was with.

Edward Dowling.

He was short and stocky. She had never seen him shaved and wasn't surprised to see his face covered with stubble and his hair unruly. The ring in his right ear would have made a pirate proud and his eyebrows would have looked good on a gorilla. His arms were covered with ugly tattoos and his fat fingers were adorned with too many rings. She could not understand what Linda saw in him.

As far as Claire was concerned, he had nothing going for him, except for his voice. It was a pleasant baritone and a woman could listen to him for hours telling his stories, providing she had her eyes closed. He'd never make a good TV host because of his looks, but he was a DJ on one of the local radio stations and quite popular.

She had never seen the other couple. At least she assumed they were a couple.

The woman was short and a little on the plump side. Her short blond hair framed a pretty face. When Claire walked into the room, the woman was laughing loudly. She stopped laughing when she saw Claire and Carmen.

"You must be Claire, Randy's girlfriend," she said, getting up.

26

Claire laughed softly, a little embarrassed by the woman's remark. "I wouldn't exactly say I'm his girlfriend," she said. "More like a good friend."

"Oh, I'm sorry. I assumed. By the way, I'm Ann."

"Hi, Ann. This is Carmen, my best friend."

"Hi Carmen. Pleased to meet you. Are you a riding instructor?"

"No, I'm not. I leave that job to Randy," Carmen said with a little laugh. "Claire and I spent the afternoon on horseback giving our horses a workout. That's why we're still wearing out outfits."

"You have horses?"

"I have one. So has Claire. Randy looks after them. The authorities frown on keeping horses in the city." She laughed again.

"I don't have a horse, but I love watching them race. So does my boyfriend. By the way, that big guy with the muscle shirt is Sid Mahony. He owns a car dealership. Mahony Enterprises."

"Maybe I should make friends with him. For my next car," Carmen said.

"Just don't get too friendly with him. He's taken." Ann broke again into that loud laugh. "I'm kidding. We're not committed to each other. By the way, are you alone? I don't see anyone else. A guy, I mean."

Randy must have heard Ann, for he came over. Looking at Carmen, he said, "David will be here shortly. He got held up with a client, but he's on the way." He turned to the others. "Let's go outside to the patio. I've got a cooler with beer out there and a

27

few bottles of wine for the ladies. Bring your glasses, though."

"I'll get us a couple," Claire said to Carmen.

"Don't bother. I'll have a beer. Don't need a glass for that. Wine makes me sleepy." She smirked. "I need to be awake for David so I can give him my full attention. He hates limp dolls that don't move. You should know."

Claire nodded. She and David had been in an intimate relationship before Randy showed an interest in her. David was a handsome guy, and Claire had really liked him. He was not a man of many words; he liked to get down to business right away. In his daily dealings with clients and his women. He wasn't much for foreplay. "Spread your legs, woman," he used to say to her. "Let a man do his job." One thing she had to admit, David was a gentle lover. He might be in a hurry to get started, but once he was inside, he took his time and he knew how to make a woman climax. Sometimes, she envied Carmen. It wasn't that Randy was no good when it came to making love. He was skilled and thoughtful, but he seemed to want more from her than she was willing to give. He never said, but she had the feeling he wanted some kind of commitment, while David only wanted to fuck, no strings attached.

David walked into the room while she was getting her glass from the cupboard. "Hi, Claire," he said, looking around. "Where is everyone?"

"On the patio." She gave him a smile. "Carmen is already waiting for you."

"She can wait." He came over and pulled her into his arm. "I've missed you," he said and kissed

28

her. At first, she pulled back, but then she returned his kiss. "You taste nice," he said, letting her go, almost reluctantly.

She ran her fingers over her lips. "What the hell was that all about?"

"I don't know," he said. "When I saw you reaching for that glass, I couldn't help but remember how you looked when you stretched your delectable naked body after we made love, like a cat, so sinewy and sexy. It was always a turn-on for me. You made me so hard I couldn't wait to take you again."

"And you did. I remember."

"Didn't I make you happy?"

"Of course, you did. You were a great lover, David, but that's in the past. I've moved on. You've got Carmen now." She chuckled. "I'm sure she gives you a good workout."

He grinned. "That she does, but she isn't you. You and I had something special."

She touched his cheek. "Maybe we did, but remember, I'm a married woman."

He sighed. "Still married to that cold fish Allan?"

Nodding, she said, "I am. He wasn't always a cold fish."

"You should divorce him, and then you can really move on."

"He'll never give me a divorce. His religion doesn't allow him to do that."

"Catholic, right? That's why I'm not a member of any church. I don't need some cleric telling me what I can or can't do. I make my own decisions. Religion is for people with no mind of their own."

29

He took her arm. "Let's join the others." He gave her a sidelong glance as they walked toward the patio door. "Any chance you and I can get together? For old time's sake, you know."

She gave him a sad smile. "I don't think that would be a good idea."

"Too bad." David let go of her arm and held the patio door open for her.

"Still the gentleman," she said with a little smile and stepped outside.

Carmen spied them and came over. "There you are," she said to David and lifted up to kiss him. Then she hooked her arm into his and pulled him toward one of the padded benches.

Claire searched for Randy and saw him talking to a young, dark-haired woman. He looked at Claire when she approached them. "I wondered what happened to you," he said.

"I talked with David for a minute. He's over there with Carmen." She pointed.

"Good, then everyone is here." He turned back to the young woman. "Tell your father to get the barbeque going. You can serve us in about half an hour, okay?"

"It'll be ready, Mister Forrest." She spoke with a heavy Spanish accent.

Randy watched her for a moment as she hurried away. "Her name is Maria. I hired her and her father a week ago. I think they're both illegals. I felt sorry for them. She'll be helping with the housekeeping. The house is getting too big for Mrs. Collins. Too much work. She's not getting any younger, either. Maria's father, Juan, was a chef in

El Salvador. He doesn't speak any English, but that doesn't matter. He's a great cook."

"She's pretty."

"Maria? Yes, she is. Jealous?"

She smiled. "Should I be?"

He bent to kiss her. "You have no reason."

"It wouldn't matter, would it? We're not married, you and I. You have no claim on me and I don't have one on you, either. We are free to do what we want, right?"

He gave her a strange look. "Are you trying to tell me something?"

"I don't know. I've been feeling restless lately. What I saw today doesn't help me sleep better."

"Are you talking about the alleged murder you think you saw being committed? I suggest you put that out of your mind, Claire. I don't really know Ron that well, but, come on, he's a cop. He's supposed to protect citizens not murder them."

"I know what I saw. I'm not some silly young teenager with a vivid imagination or an old lady with cataract eyes."

He embraced her and pulled her close. Looking into her eyes, he said, "Even if what you think is true, there is nothing you can do about it. Should you somehow pursue this, it will be a useless and frustrating exercise. Who will believe you? It's your word against the word of a cop. And let's not forget the guy who was with him. He will obviously back up Ron. Forget this, Claire. You'll only drive yourself crazy." He kissed her gently.

She put her arms around his neck and clung to him. When they separated, she whispered, "You are right, Randy. I don't need any more stress. I want you to make love to me right now."

"Now?" He laughed, stroking her hair. "You may notice I have guests to entertain. I can't just leave, even though I want you badly."

"Forget about them. They won't even miss us." She clung to him, pressing her lower body against him. She could feel his penis hardening in his pants. "I can see you're ready. So am I."

He pushed her away, gently. "I'm always ready for you, but I don't want to rush this. Once everyone had a few drinks and once we're done eating, we'll go upstairs." He smiled. "You know how these evenings usually end up. They'll all be busy doing their own thing. We'll have all the time in the world. All night if you want. Okay?"

She made a face. "Okay, but I want you to pay special attention to my needs, promise."

"Don't I always?"

"Most of the time." She gave him an impish smile. "I think I'll fill this empty glass I've been carrying. I need a drink."

"Go ahead. It'll relax you. I'll go and check up on the steaks."

She filled her glass halfway from a bottle of Merlot and turned to join the others when the short woman walked up to refill her glass. "I hear you own a horse," she said to Claire.

Claire nodded. "His name is Black Lightening. Don't ask me why. That's what his previous owner called him. Randy bought him for me from a breeder he knows. Apparently, Black Lightening comes from a line of racing horses."

"You've raced him?"

32

"Oh, heavens no." Claire laughed. "Not on a racetrack, anyway. I let him run on flat stretch of land, though."

"Aren't you scared he might throw you?"

"He hasn't yet. He doesn't buck if that's what you mean. Have you been thrown off a horse?"

"No. The ones I've been riding were gentle mares, and then only when I was with a group going on a trail ride. It must be fun to ride a running horse but scary, too. For me, anyway."

Claire gave a little shrug. "Randy taught me. I'm sure you're aware he is a riding instructor. He gives lessons."

Ann gave a little nod. "I never seem to have time for these things. Too busy with my business."

"What do you do?"

"I'm a wedding planner. It takes all my time, but I enjoy it." She tilted her head. "I know it's none of my business, but have you and Randy made plans already."

"To get married?"

"Have you?"

Claire turned her head to look away for a moment. "I'm already married," she said with a low voice.

"I don't understand. I thought you and Randy were more than just friends. What am I missing?"

"I'm married to another man."

"Oh." There was an awkward pause. "I suppose you're in an unhappy marriage," Ann finally said. "Am I right?"

"You are."

"How long have you been married, if I may ask?"

"Four years. We were happy once."

"That's how all marriages start. I know about that, because I was married for a while. It didn't work out. It happens. Take my advice, don't stay in an unhappy marriage. Get out before you get too old. You're still young enough to start fresh. As for me, I'll stay single. I have my job and no use for a husband."

"How about that muscle-bound guy with you?" Claire smiled.

"Sid?" Ann laughed that hearty laugh. "He gives me what I need, if you know what I mean. As for marrying him, no chance. He isn't the first one after my divorce and he won't be the last. I like variety in the food I eat, the wine I drink, and the men I screw."

Claire laughed. "The problem with that is you're not on a steady diet. Too much lean time in-between."

"That's true, but you enjoy it twice as much when it happens." She looked back at Sid. "I'm planning for it to happen tonight. It's been over a week now since we've gone out. I'm going a little stir-crazy." Laying her hand on Claire's arm in a familiar gesture, she said with a wink, "Don't let an opportunity slip by to find pleasure. Enjoy every moment. Time passes too quickly. Now I must get back to good old Sidney, before he looks for someone else." She laughed. "Of course, there is nobody else unless your girlfriend seeks greener pastures."

"Carmen?" Claire chuckled. "She's quite happy with David."

Ann waved her hand and walked away. Claire watched her, feeling jealous.

'That woman seems happy with her life. I wish I could be like that." Her attention moved to Carmen, who sat in one of the couches with David. They appeared to be in deep conversation. Both of them laughed at something funny one of them must have said. Carmen was another woman who seemed happy. She had been through three husbands. That's how she became rich and independent. She didn't need another man to make her happy, and yet, here she was flirting with David. Claire wouldn't put it past her, if she ended up getting married to David. In a way, Carmen was a fortune hunter.

She turned when she heard Randy. "Okay, peoples. May I ask you to take your seats at the table, please? The food is being served and best consumed when still hot. The steaks look delicious, done to perfection by my new cook Carlos. He's actually a chef and the best in his field. I'm fortunate to have him. Bring your filled glasses or full bottles, whatever you prefer. Everything else is on the table, except for the steaks. They'll be served when everyone is seated."

Claire strolled over to the round table and chose a chair, waiting for the others.

Carmen joined her a few moments later. "It smells and looks delicious," she said. "And the wine is great, too."

"I thought you were drinking beer. How many bottles have you consumed?"

"Probably too much." Carmen giggled. "Wine I mean. I changed my mind about the beer."

"Didn't you say wine makes you sleepy?"

"It does, but David likes it when I'm a little tipsy. Wine works better for that. According to him, I lose all my inhibitions." Carmen giggled again. "He doesn't know I don't have any." She turned to watch David sit down beside her. "There you are."

The others also took their seats. Before Sid sat down, he held up his bottle of beer, "To our gracious host Randy. Thanks for inviting me. Perhaps I can repay the favor and sell all of you one of my vehicles. I'll give you a good deal."

"You must forgive him," Ann said with a chuckle. "He can't help himself. He was born a car salesman. According to his mother, before he was born, he drummed a message in Morse code saying he wasn't coming out unless his crib was in the shape of a car."

Everyone laughed. The women lifted their glass and the men their bottle. "To Randy."

"Don't make a big deal out of it. I enjoy entertaining my friends." Randy lifted his own bottle. "I'm glad you all came. It gets a little lonely sometimes out here on the ranch."

"You need a good woman to keep you company," Linda said. Her gaze rested on Claire. "Are you still with that bore—what's his name?"

"His name is Allan and he isn't a bore. He's a successful business man and my husband." Claire felt defensive. She didn't know why.

"And yet, here you are, ready to fuck another man."

Claire rose from her chair abruptly, spilling her wine onto the table. She turned and ran toward the house but didn't go inside, just stood there, fists on her side. Tears of Anger and guilt welled up inside

36

her. She didn't need anyone telling her what she was doing was wrong. The death of Andy wasn't Allan's fault. As a good wife, she should stand by her husband's side and comfort him in his grief, no matter how long it took for him to get over his loss.

Someone touched her shoulder. "That wasn't called for." It was Carmen. "Don't take it so seriously. She's drunk. You know how she gets when she had too much to drink. Just ignore her."

Claire turned and clung to her friend for a moment. Wiping her tears, she said, "The problem is she's right. I'm not a good wife. Aren't a husband and a wife supposed to support each other in good times and in bad times? Isn't that what we promise when we get married?"

"Those are old-fashioned ideas. Things change. Remember when they also said that a woman is supposed to obey her husband? What a bunch of crap! This is the twenty-first century. Wake up, girl. Allan isn't supporting you, so why should you support him? He ignores you. He doesn't care for your feelings and most likely doesn't love you anymore." She took Claire's arm. "Come back to the table and forget what that bitch said. Don't spoil the evening for the rest of us. Be the bigger person."

Claire let Carmen pull her toward the table. She was surprised when she saw Linda getting up and approaching her. "Listen, Claire, I was way out of line with that. I shouldn't have said it. I don't know why I did. I'm sorry. It's the wine. It makes me say things I regret later. Forgive me?"

Claire stared at her, at a loss as how she should react. "You are right," she finally said, "you were out of line. If you knew my situation you wouldn't run off your mouth like that. Maybe what I'm doing is wrong, but you have no right to judge me. Nobody has. I'm the only one who can do that. Do me a favor and don't talk to me for the rest of the evening."

Linda lifted both hand in a defensive gesture. "Okay, just don't bite off my head." She stumbled back to her seat.

"As you can see, she's drunk. By tomorrow morning she probably won't remember any of this." Carmen bent close to Claire's ear and whispered, "She needs to be drunk to fuck that ape she's with."

Despite her anger, Claire had to chuckle. "You always know the right things to say, Carmen. You're a good friend. I hope we can stay friends forever."

"There is no reason we can't. Come on, let's have some fun."

When she took her seat again beside Randy, he put his hand over hers. "Are you alright?"

She nodded. "I'll be fine. After another glass of wine."

"I had Maria refill your glass. I hope the choice is okay. I didn't know what you were drinking."

"Thank you. All your wines are good. Whatever it is will be fine. As long as it's red." She took a long sip and put the glass down with a sigh. "I'm ready for that juicy steak you promised."

"I'll drink to that," Carmen said beside her and drained her glass.

Conversation was light for the rest of the meal, except when Dowling and Mahony got into an argument about the price of cars and trucks. "Why are trucks more expensive than cars?" Dowling wanted to know.

"Because they are in high demand these days," Mahony explained.

"In the country, maybe, but not in the city," Dowling argued.

They carried on for a little while. Claire tried to tune it out. She found conversations like that boring. She turned to Carmen. "I'm going to the bathroom. You want to come?"

"Okay."

Carmen held on to Claire. "I think I drank too much."

Claire giggled. "Me, too."

When they returned to the table, everyone had moved back to the couches. Randy came up to her. "Come, let's dance."

She rose and moved into his arms. Randy had turned up the music just loud enough to make it enjoyable. Despite his age, he was an old-fashioned guy who didn't like modern music blaring over giant speakers. He preferred instrumental music. Saxophone, violins and guitars, as long as they weren't electric guitars. She shared his taste most of the time, but she didn't mind listening to soft rock and jazz.

"You're not your usual happy self today," he observed.

"I know. It hasn't been a good week for me. What happened today didn't exactly lift my mood."

"Remember what I said about that. Push it out of your mind. Come, let's go upstairs." He chuckled. "Now nobody will miss us."

She looked at the other couples. Only Ann and Mahony were dancing. Linda and Dowling were still on the couch in a deep embrace. She didn't see Carmen and David.

"Okay," she said and followed him upstairs.

At the top of the stairs he pulled her close. "Let's go into the bedroom."

"We can go, but I'm not really in the mood anymore," she said. "Sorry."

"That's okay. We can just talk for a while."

Randy's bedroom was huge. On the high ceiling, an old chandelier lit up the room with subdued light. The many crystals hanging from the glass arms and the bulbs could use at least some dusting to make them sparkle again. The furniture was old and outdated, but everything was solid wood. Four intricately carved massive posts and a tall headboard adorned the big bed. The only thing new on the bed was the mattress. It was firm, something Claire could attest to. This wouldn't be the first time she'd spend a night in Randy's bedroom.

"I would offer you a drink," he said with a little smile, "but you've probably had enough already."

"Maybe too much." She kicked off her shoes and sat on the edge of the bed.

He sat beside her and laid an arm around her shoulder. "I hate to see you this way. A beautiful woman like you should be cheerful and laughing all the time. If you were my wife, I'd always make sure you're happy."

"I know you would, but I'm not your wife. Too bad we didn't meet before I met Allan."

"From what I hear you were quite a party-girl. You may not even have given me a second look."

"Maybe not. Laid-back guys like you didn't inspire me."

"How about now? What changed your mind?"

"You." She pulled his head down and kissed him. "Let's get undressed and snuggle," she whispered. "You never know what can happen."

He drew back the covers and, naked, they slipped under them. "Hold me tight," she said, shivering. "I need to feel your warm body against mine. I'm just a little bit chilly."

"I'll try to make you hot." He laughed and kissed her breasts.

Closing her eyes, she enjoyed his lips and tongue on her breasts and trembled when he moved down to her belly.

He touched her mound and let his finger caress her slit. "That feels nice," she whispered and moaned when he pushed his finger into her. He replaced his finger with his mouth and gently licked her clitoris. She cried out softly and grabbed his hair. "Yes," she moaned, "that's it...oh my god...that feels so nice...don't wait any longer. I need to feel you inside me."

He moved between her spread legs. She felt his hard penis touching her belly. He was not in a hurry as he rubbed it slowly back and forth between her pussy lips. She lifted up and moved her lower body, trying to capture him inside her. "Don't tease," she sobbed. "Push it in...now, please."

He chuckled when she grabbed his penis and frantically guided it between her labia, pushing up against him. Then, with a satisfied grunt, he finally entered her and slowly pushed his engorged member into her dripping pussy.

She felt it slide in with agonizing slowness, filling her completely, and she gave a loud cry when he was lodged inside her.

He moved in and out of her with a steady rhythm for a long time, bringing her to a number of orgasms. She writhed beneath him, her breath coming in loud gasps, as she floated in a sea of pure pleasure. "Don't come yet," she begged when she felt him falter in his movements, but he moaned, "I can't hold it any longer. I'm coming…now!" He grabbed her buttocks and held her still. Expelling his breath loudly, he let out a series of hoarse shouts, shuddering in her embrace. She felt his throbbing penis pump inside her and held him until he relaxed between her cradling thighs, wishing he would have lasted just a little bit longer.

He lay on top of her, his breath rattling in his throat.

"You're getting heavy," she said after a while.

"Sorry." He moved over and lay beside her, still breathing hard. "You sure gave me some workout," he said after a while. "I haven't seen you this wild for a long time."

"I guess I needed this more than I thought. "She turned to look at him. "Did you mind?"

"Mind?" He chuckled. "Hell, this was the best one in a long time. For a while, I thought you were going to crush my penis with that hot, tight pussy of yours. And the way you squeezed me at the end. Wow, I was hoping you wouldn't suck my blood. Did you turn into some kind of vampire?"

42

"Oh you." She slapped him on the shoulder. "Now you embarrass me."

"I didn't mean to. That was a compliment." He bent over her and kissed her. "I wish we could do this more often. Like every night."

She sighed. "You wouldn't last. You'd lose weight and shrivel up." She touched his nose with her finger. "Don't think you're done for the night. I'll stay with you until morning. The night is long and as soon as you have recuperated, I want that big pleasure maker inside me again. And don't argue."

"Who's arguing? I was hoping you'd say that. What about Carmen?"

"That won't be a problem. I told her on the way here that I was going to stay overnight. You'll have to take me home, though."

"I won't have time for that, because I have a number of students coming in the morning, but I'll let Larry drive you home." He reached for her and pulled her into his embrace.

Chapter Three

Allan was home when Larry dropped her off in front of her house. Usually, he didn't even seem to notice her presence, but this time he met her by the door when she walked in. "Where have you been?"

She gave him a surprised look. "What do you care? Why this sudden interest?"

"I'm always interested where you are. When I came home last night, you weren't here. Where were you?"

"You may remember I have a horse. I went to the ranch with Carmen to do some riding."

"That wasn't Carmen dropping you off. Who was that guy? Are you sleeping with him?"

"That was Larry Collins. He is the son of Randy's housekeeper. I'm certainly not sleeping with him."

"You stayed overnight? What happened to Carmen?"

"She left early. I wanted to spend more time with my horse. It got too late to drive home so I stayed overnight."

"In Randy's house."

"Where else? He's got a number of guest rooms. Some of his students stay overnight sometimes. What is your problem?"

He made a dismissing motion with his hand. "Forget it. You've become so damn bitchy. I'm meeting a client tonight, here at the house. This is a million-dollar deal, and I want to make sure everything goes smoothly. I want you to be here and play hostess. Can you do that or do you have any other, more important, business to take care of?" His last words dripped with sarcasm.

"What about Carol? Will she be here to serve your guests or are you expecting me to be the maid?"

"She'll be here, but I want you to look sexy and serve the drinks. Show off your boobs. That shouldn't be a problem, should it?"

"I'm surprised you remember I have boobs. You certainly don't notice them."

"Don't start that again. Sometimes I think you have no sympathy for other people's grief. Looking at your breasts is the last thing on my mind these days."

"It would be nice if you would look at me once in a while, Allan. You've been ignoring me for two years now. How long until you realize that life goes on. Life is for the living. The dead don't give a crap."

"Like I said no sympathy. It's always about you. Everything turns around you. Sometimes, you just make me sick."

"Keep that up and I'll leave right now again!"

"Any other time I wouldn't care, but tonight you stay home." He spoke sharply. "I want you to look your best. Smile and pretend you are the perfect wife. That is the image I want to see. Understood?"

"If you say so, Master Belmont. I am your obedient servant," she said mockingly and made a bow. "I shall not embarrass you."

"Don't be stupid. You're only embarrassing yourself." He turned and stalked away.

She looked after him and pushed out her tongue, annoyed and angry at his attitude—and herself. She realized there was no more love for him left inside her. Climbing up the staircase, she went to her room and decided to take a shower. While she undressed slowly, her thoughts drifted to Randy. Their lovemaking had been gentle and fierce at the same time. Did she love him? She didn't know. She liked him well enough. He was handsome with his six-foot-high frame, athletic, and always in a good mood. If she somehow had the opportunity to marry him, would she? She couldn't answer that. It didn't matter anyway. It was just a hypothetical question.

She felt better after the shower. Her phone rang as she was on her way out into the backyard. It was Carmen. "Hey, girlfriend. You've made it home. How did things go?"

"As expected," Claire chuckled into the phone. "I'm still tingling. I got home about an hour ago. Thanks for picking me up yesterday. I needed that. How did things turn out with you and David?"

Carmen laughed. "You know David. He doesn't fool around, but it was great. He knows how to please a woman, that's for sure. I'm meeting him for dinner this weekend. After that, we'll drive down to Mellarny. We'll spend a couple of days at the beach and, you know…"

"I guess I won't see you for a few days."

"I'll give you a call as soon as I'm back. Well, gotta go. I want to drive to Reedman's to buy myself a new bathing suit and an evening dress. I need to look good for David. You want to come along as an advisor?"

46

"Sorry. Can't. I have to get things ready for tonight. Allan's got an important client coming over. He wants me to be the good hostess."

"Sounds interesting. Are you two making up?"

Claire snorted. "There is no chance, aside from a miracle, of that ever happening. The time for that has come and gone. No, he wants me to be the charming and dumb wife to secure the deal. I'm supposed to look sexy."

"Then do. Put it on strong. Show him what he's missing."

"Maybe I'll go naked. Or I could always wear that nearly transparent fishnet outfit I bought for our first anniversary. That should be sexy enough."

"Remember what we discussed? Who knows? This might be your first assignment in your mission 'Operation Pussy'. Wouldn't it be ironic? And Allan would be instrumental in orchestrating his own downfall."

"You are a crazy woman and devious to boot. Your thinking is completely different from that of a normal person. I didn't know I was on a mission." Claire smiled, even though Carmen couldn't see her.

"You are, but you need help. I'm that person. Let's put it this way—I'm the architect. I do all the planning and you execute the plan. There is no way you can lose. Be your sexiest tonight and follow the clues. That is your mission. I'll get in touch with you again next week. Burn your phone after this conversation in case somebody is tracking you."

Claire laughed. "You are just so silly. I'm glad I have you in my life. You make it easier for me to get over the hurdles I'm facing these days. I love

47

you. Have a good time with David, but don't wear him out."

"I'm planning to do just that." Carmen's laughter stopped abruptly when she shut off her phone.

Claire spent the afternoon making sure there was enough liquor in the cabinet. She also put a couple bottles of white wine into the fridge and checked to see if there were enough bottles of different red wines on the wine rack. She still knew what Allan wanted, even though they hadn't entertained guests for the past two years. It almost brought back memories of happier times.

When Carol showed up, Claire told her to prepare a few hors d'oeuvres and serve them as soon as the guests arrived. After that, she went up to her room to search for a suitable outfit to wear. She chose a short skirt that showed off her slim legs and a blouse with buttons. She could open them as the situation demanded. No bra.

After the doorbell rang, she went to the door to personally greet the guests. Allan had not told her anything about his prospective new client, and she didn't know what to expect. She saw two men. The one standing in front of the door was of average height, slim, clean-shaven. His eyes were slightly slanted. He wore a dark suit under a long black coat. His head was bare.

He made a slight bow. "Good evening. I am Kaito Tanaka. Please, tell your employer, Mister Belmont, I have arrived." Even though he spoke with a slight accent, his English was impeccable.

"Good evening, Mister Tanaka. We've been expecting you. Come on in. By the way, I am Claire Belmont, Mister Belmont's wife."

"My apologies." He made another bow. "So sorry. Pleased to meet you, Missis Belmont."

"No apology necessary." She gave him a smile. "I'm pleased to meet you also. Come in. The family room is to your left."

As Tanaka stepped across the threshold, she looked at the second man and took a step backward. She recognized him immediately. The last time she saw him, he and a cop, whose name, according to Randy, was Ron Salsky, dragged a third man out of the water. A man they probably murdered.

Before she could say anything, the man said, "I'm Mohan Bakshi. I'm Mister Tanaka's lawyer. Nice to make your acquaintance, Missis Belmont."

There was no indication in his manners that he recognized her, and she wondered about that. Either he was a good actor or he actually did not know who she was. He entered the house and looked around. "Beautiful home you have, Missis Belmont. Perhaps someday I can meet the architect who designed it. I've always liked modern houses."

"I'm afraid I don't know who designed this house. My husband bought it only a couple of years ago through a real estate agency. Maybe he knows. You can talk to him."

"I just might." He followed Tanaka into the family room.

She walked slowly, not being in a hurry to join them, her thoughts occupied with the strange coincidence to see the man, who she was positive had committed murder, in her home. She could hear

49

Allan talking to Tanaka. They both laughed at some joke one of them must have made.

When she walked into the room, Allan looked at her. "There you are, Sweetheart. Be so kind and bring Mister Tanaka a glass of green tea and a glass of white wine for Mister Bakshi."

"Okay, Honey. I'll be back in a jiffy." She turned around and walked away, putting a little swing into her hips. He wanted sexy? She'll give him sexy. In the kitchen, Carol was busy fixing hors d'oeuvres. "Boil a pot of water and make green tea," she told Carol. "Our guest is a tea drinker. He's lucky I also drink the occasional cup of green tea, otherwise he'd be out of luck."

She got the bottle of white wine out of the fridge and filled a glass. Putting it onto a tray, she went into Allan's office and took out a bottle of Scotch. Pouring some into a glass, she added a cube of ice. That's the way Allan liked his Scotch. Then she went back into the kitchen.

Carol had already prepared the green tea, but it needed to steep for a couple of minutes. Claire used the time to sip on a glass of white wine. She didn't see any reason why she shouldn't. After all, this was her home.

As soon as the tea was finished brewing, she went back into the family room. Allan and his guests were sitting around the glass table in one corner.

Tanaka nodded when she put the tea in front him. "Thank you, Missis Belmont."

She handed Bakshi the glass with wine and then she gave Allan his Scotch.

50

"You are a lucky man, Mister Belmont, to have such a beautiful home and an even more beautiful wife. She seems very devoted to you. That is admirable." Tanaka looked at Claire when he said that. She had opened her blouse a little to show the top of her bare breasts and it was more than obvious what he admired.

"Yes, she is beautiful," Allan said.

Claire didn't know if he meant the house or her. Probably the house.

"We'll be fine for a little while," Allan told Claire. "Go check on Carol and tell her to serve the hors d'oeuvres. I'll call you when I need you again."

"I'll be waiting for your summons," she said with a sweet voice. "After all, that is my wifely duty." She left the family room, swinging her hips even more.

She smiled when she heard Tanaka say, "Your wife is quite seductive. I would watch her, Mister Belmont." He laughed. "And now, shall we get down to business?"

* * *

Allan was actually in a good mood the next morning. "Have breakfast with me," he said. She usually went to the gym at this time, but she joined him at the breakfast table. She didn't remember the last time that happened.

"Things went well last night," Allan said. "We've signed a contract and it will be profitable for our company. My father will be pleased."

"His lawyer is a murderer," Claire said.

51

"What the hell are you talking about?"

"I saw him and another guy, a cop by the name of Ron Salsky, drown a guy."

"When is this to have happened?" He gave her a challenging look.

"A couple of days ago when I went riding. Carmen saw it too."

"Have you two been drinking when you saw this alleged murder? Perhaps even high on drugs?"

"No. Both of us were quite sober. We don't consume alcohol when we go riding, and you should know, I don't do drugs." She leaned back in her chair. "I can see you won't believe me, but I stand by what I saw. My advice to you is stay away from this Tanaka and his lawyer. They're not even Americans."

His laughter mocked her. "What do I care if they're Americans or not. Business is business. In fact, there is more money to be made in international trade than in our own country. I need this deal, but what do you care? All you do is lazy around all day long, go riding and have fun. Who knows what you and your girlfriend saw. Tanaka is a successful businessman with more money than he knows what to do with. He also has connections to other companies and he hinted he may send more business my way. This deal can turn into a gold mine for us. Don't screw it up with this crazy talk about murders. By the way, did you report what you think you saw to the police?"

"No, we didn't. We have no proof to substantiate what we saw. Randy advised me not to pursue it."

"Randy advised you. That's nice. What else is he advising you about? Our marriage?"

"Why? Is our marriage in trouble?" She stared at him with a challenging expression.

"Don't act in this stupid manner. You and I spend less and less time together. We never talk, and you're barely home."

"Wow!" Claire didn't know what to say to that. "Talk? All you want to talk about is Andy."

"That's right. Because he is on my mind all the time. I can't get him out of my head. Of course, you wouldn't understand that. Just imagine your sister would have been murdered. Would you not miss her? Would you not grief?"

"Naturally I would grief, but not at the expense of everyone around me. I would certainly not neglect you and I would hope you support me in my sorrow. Neither would I mope around for two years."

"I'm not surprised to hear you say that. You'd expect me to stand by your side, something you don't do."

"I tried, Allan. I really tried. Yesterday, you accused me of having no sympathy. I have only so much sympathy inside me." A sudden compassionate feeling toward him made her say it with a softer voice, "Do you know that this is the longest and most civilized conversation we've had in a long time?"

"If you'd stay home more often, we would have more opportunities to communicate." His voice carried nothing but accusation.

"I cannot sit home and feel pity for you and me day after day, night after night." Her eyes filled with

53

tears. "I need your love, Allan. I need for you to take me into your arms, tell me you love me. I need to share your bed at night, feel your body against mine. I'm longing for the love and passion we once shared. Is that so much to ask?"

He hit the table top with his flat hand and got up. "Here we go again, Claire. That's what it's all about with you—fucking! That's all you ever wanted. You don't give a crap about my feelings and what I want. The last thing on my mind right now is to fall between your spread legs and listen to your moans and shouts as you satisfy your craving. You're like a bitch in constant heat, but I'm not a fucking male dog. Why don't you buy yourself a damn vibrator and go at it!"

She sat stunned by his stinging words. "You are cruel, Allan," she said with a teary voice.

"Ah, fuck you. Don't start crying now. I can't stand that." He walked away without looking back.

She stared at his receding back, her tears flowing freely now. She realized their marriage had reached a point from which there was no return. Reconciliation was out of reach now. It was something she had to face and accept. Wiping her tears, she decided to go the gym.

Most of the people in the gym were women. She knew some of them, but she had never made any close connections with any. There were a few regulars, but the majority of them came only for a short time and either found exercising too much work, it didn't help them lose weight, or it was too time-consuming.

Clair found it helped her to conquer the inner battle she was fighting and it kept her in shape. She liked the way her body looked and she wanted to keep her good figure as long as possible. Not to mention the health benefits attached to regular exercising.

First, she went through her routine of stretching and then she got onto the treadmill. She didn't pay any attention to the treadmills beside her. One of them was occupied and the other one was empty. When someone stepped onto the empty one, she saw the figure from the corner of her eye and noticed it was a man but didn't look any closer.

Then another man appeared in front of her treadmill and put his hands on the console. Looking up, she nearly lost her balance and almost slipped off.

"Hello, Missis Belmont," said a familiar voice.

She stopped the track and stared at him. "What do you want?"

The man gave her a wide smile. "Is that any way to greet an old friend?"

"We are not old friends, Mister Bakshi. You are a man doing business with my husband. That doesn't make us friends."

"Don't try to fool me, Claire. I know you recognized me."

"So what if I recognized you? I can't help it. I have a good memory for faces."

"That may not always be a good thing. As it happens, I also remember faces."

"You pretended not to recognize me."

"Same goes for you. For a little while I was hoping you really didn't know who I was. It would have been better for both of us."

"How did you know I was in this club?"

He chuckled. "Last night, you displayed your body quite freely. I have to admit, you did look sexy. Anyway, it didn't take much guessing to know that nobody gets a trim body like yours without spending considerable time in a gym. A few calls to the clubs in the area, and it didn't take long to locate you."

"I thought member lists where private. I guess I was wrong."

"Did you forget that my buddy Ron is a cop? You'd be surprised how freely people talk when a member of the police department calls. By the way, you can ask him yourself. He's exercising right beside you."

Claire turned her head to look at the treadmill to the right. Sure enough, there was Salsky walking at a good pace. He waved and smiled when he saw her looking at him. Then he slowed down and stepped off.

"Surprised to see me, Claire?"

"I was hoping never to see your face again." She gave him a defiant look. "Why are you here? The both of you?"

"That's quite simple. We want to find out what you think you saw down by the lake that day?"

"Simple? I saw three men standing in the water. One was submerged while the other two seemed to hold him down. That's what I saw."

"We told you he hit his head, fell into the water and drowned. Don't believe it? What's your theory?"

"I don't believe he drowned all by himself. I think you murdered him, that's my theory." She knew it was the wrong thing to say, but for some

56

reason she was angry that they had the gall to come into her gym, invade her privacy, and then try to intimidate her.

Salsky came close to her and looked into her eyes. "Have you and your girlfriend talked to anyone about this theory of yours?"

She lifted her shoulders. "Maybe we have or maybe we haven't," she said haughtily, but with false bravado.

Salsky came even closer. She could feel his breath on her face. "I'd be careful spreading false rumors," he said in a low voice only she could hear. "There might be unpleasant consequences. For one thing, you wouldn't want your husband to lose that new profitable client of his, would you now?"

She shrank back when he grabbed her chin with his thumb and forefinger. "How about if a little accident leaves your pretty face with a bunch of ugly scars? You'd be surprised what a tiny, old-fashioned razor blade can do in just a few seconds with smooth skin as soft as yours. I'd hate to even think about that."

She shook off his hand and took a couple of steps backward. "Are you threatening me? I can report you to your superiors."

He laughed and turned to his buddy. "Did you hear that, Mohan? Missis Belmont here wants to report me to my superiors. You're a lawyer. What do you think about that idea?"

"I'd say it is a stupid idea. You're a decorated top-cop with a reputation of being honorable and above suspicion. You have a great relationship with your chief. You're respected in your department. Nobody would even believe a word she'd say."

"I'll find somebody who will believe me. Nobody is above suspicion. I'll report you to Internal Affairs. I could go to the media or the FBI."

"The FBI! Wow! Now you're really reaching. The FBI doesn't worry about petty local crimes. You're reading too many crime novels, Claire." Salsky's chuckle was almost cheerful. "As far as Internal Affairs goes—good luck there. The chief is a good friend of mine. Being a civilian, you may not know this, but we cops stick together, and a civilian's accusation against a cop is rarely taken seriously."

Claire clenched her fists. "I have friends in the press. I'll go public."

"You do that and you'll have a lawsuit against you for falsely accusing a good cop so fast it'll make your head spin," Bakshi warned. "I'm a good lawyer and I barely loose a case."

"You're bluffing." Claire felt angry and helpless. "I want you both to leave right now. If you don't go, I'll call Security and tell them you accosted me."

"Don't be so intense. Nobody accosted you. We talked to Security on the way in. I told them I'm your cousin. You and I are almost like brother and sister." Salsky grinned. "I also told them you have a bit of a temper and a flair for the melodramatic. You also suffer from paranoia. That's the reason I sort of keep an eye on you." He spread his hands. "They understood. Cousins that are close do that for each other."

Claire spat. "My father-in-law is an important man with great influence. I'll talk to him. He'll listen."

58

Salsky came close again. "You don't seem to get it, Claire. Let me give you one last warning. If you are trying to make trouble, we'll find you. Same goes for your girlfriend. Women disappear every day without a trace. How would you like to spend the rest of your days in Saudi Arabia? I hear there are openings in some sheik's harem. My buddy Mohan has friends in Saudi Arabia who could arrange that."

"Go!" She almost screamed it. Then she turned and ran toward the changing rooms, shaking with anger and fear. She cursed the day she saw those two men. They were dangerous, and she believed they would have no qualms killing her if they figured she was a threat to them.

She spent a long time in the shower trying to calm her nerves. Before she left the gym, she went to the front and told the girl at the reception counter never to let anyone into the exercise room before talking to her, no matter who they said they were.

Chapter Four

Some people falsely believe being rich and living in a big house is the ultimate living experience, a dream come true, especially when you're a woman married to a rich man. You don't have to worry about work or anything else. You can lie in the sun all day long, take a dip in your private swimming pool, drink the finest wines or cocktails, and talk with friends on the phone without worrying about wasting time. After all, there is always the next day where you can go shopping or just go for a drive in your fancy car.

Claire wished she could tell all those people who actually believed that how wrong they were.

She had all that and was bored out of her mind. What good was a life like that without the love of a man? The only true friend she had was Carmen. All the other women she knew where either too old or too young. Some were happily married, some weren't. Some spent their time playing tennis or golfing or with other activities. A few even had their own careers.

She never had a career. The only real job she ever held was working for a few years as a clerk in the Bank of Rocktown where she grew up. All the other jobs were dead-end jobs and mostly part time. She had been a cheerleader with the Rocktown Rockets and enjoyed a variety of sports. No careers there.

She looked at herself in the mirror and sighed. "You should have become a model," she told her image. "You could wear beautiful clothes, travel and let men admire you. Of course, many of them would be rich, old men who would try to get you into their bed. Not the ideal life I would want, either."

She picked up her cell and checked it for calls, hoping Carmen would at least send her a text, telling her she'd changed her mind and wasn't going away with David for a few days after all and she'd be right over to spend a little time with her. But there was nothing on the phone. Nobody else ever left messages, not even Allan. Especially not Allan.

When the phone actually rang, it took her by surprise and she almost didn't answer it. When she did, she received another surprise. The call was from someone she never expected to hear from again.

"Claire?"

"Yes?"

"This is Roy Sanders. Remember me?"

She didn't answer for a moment as memories flooded back.

"Claire? Are you there?"

"Yes, I'm here. How did you get my number?"

He chuckled. "Easy. I called your parents. Is something wrong?"

"Why do you ask?"

"Your voice. It doesn't sound the way I remembered. You know—bubbly, carefree."

"People change, Roy. I'm older now. Wiser and more mature." She tried to make it sound light and funny but knew she didn't succeed. "I'm just surprised to hear from you, that's all. Is there a special reason you're calling?"

"No special reason. I talked with Millie Cummings the other day and somehow your name came up and we wondered how you were doing. I know you're playing in the big league now. I mean, being married to a multimillionaire and stuff. Perhaps you don't even want to talk to common folk like us." He laughed softly.

"Don't be silly, Roy. I will never forget my roots. Neither will I forget you. We have too much history."

"I'll say. After all, you and I were engaged for more than three years. I miss you."

She felt the tightness in her throat. She wanted to say 'I miss you, too' but instead she said, "How can you still miss me? We were young and it's been so long since then."

"Eight years since you left Rocktown, and me. Eight years, Claire. That isn't so long ago. I'd like to see you. Can we meet somewhere?"

She hesitated. It may not be a good idea to meet with the only man she ever truly loved, the man she left to move to the big city. It would only open old wounds and end with nothing but heartaches. "When?" she said, against her better judgement.

"Tonight."

"How can we meet tonight? I can't just jump on a plane to meet you."

"You won't have to. I'm in town on a conference. Meet me at my hotel. I'm at the Royal Crown. How about eight o'clock?"

"I don't know, Roy. It wouldn't right."

"Why not? Just to catch up and swap some stories. Come on, Claire, don't say no. We'll have dinner, that's all. Tell you husband you're meeting with an old girlfriend from home."

"My husband went on a business trip. He won't be home for at least three days. That won't be a problem."

"Then what is the problem? It'll be fun."

She stared at her image in the mirror. 'That's right, Claire. What is the problem? You're all alone in this big house. Carmen is gone for a few days. What harm can it do to meet with Roy? Maybe it'll do you good to see a friendly face from the past.'

"Alright," she said. "I'll be there, but only for a short time."

"Great. I'm looking forward to seeing you again. See you at eight."

As the hours passed, she went from being anxious to apprehensive, wondering if it was a good idea to meet with the man she nearly married. She almost had in mind to call the hotel and cancel the meeting, but she didn't.

The Royal Crown was about two hours away and she got there shortly after seven-thirty. She felt nervous and hesitant, not knowing how either of them would react. To calm her nerves, she looked for the bar to have a drink. When she entered the lounge, she saw a man sitting at the bar and froze. Even after all these years, she had no trouble recognizing his large frame. As the Captain of the Rocktown Rockets he had been the dream of all the girls. He could have had any one of them, but he chose her.

And she had left him for the big city.

She almost walked out again, losing her nerve suddenly, when he turned around and looked her way. She couldn't hear him above the music, but she read his lips.

"Claire?"

Then he got up and walked toward her. The years dropped away like sheets from a calendar with every step he took and she was back again in Rocktown, back in the diner they used to meet. Before he reached her, she rushed forward and flung herself into his arms. Looking up at him with tears in her eyes, she whispered, "Roy oh Roy, I've missed you so much."

He bent down to kiss her and she held him close, wanting to stay like that forever. All her problems seemed to have vanished. She felt free and happy.

But it only lasted a moment. Reality hit her like a sledgehammer, brought her back down to Earth when he released her. Dropping her arms, she stepped back and gave him an apologetic smile. "Sorry about that." She wiped her cheeks with one finger. "I've been going through some rough times lately. Seeing you must have triggered all that pent-up frustration."

He smiled. "I've missed you, too, Claire. I should have never let you go." He took her arm. "Come, I've reserved a table. Let's have dinner and talk."

When he held her chair and waited until she sat down, she said, "You haven't forgotten how to be a gentleman. Not many men do that anymore."

He took his seat and chuckled. "I've been called old-fashioned, but my grandfather always

64

said 'when a man doesn't treat a woman with respect, he is nothing but a boor and does not deserve her admiration. Neither does he deserve the respect of other men.' He was a gentleman and was revered in the community for his integrity and treatment of others, no matter their social standing. I believe in his principles and I try to live by them."

"You are a rare specimen of a man," Claire said with a little smile. "My parents always liked that about you."

"I'm not so sure if your mother was overly fond of me." He laughed. "She told me one time I was too handsome and not really husband-material."

"My mom said that to you? I didn't know that."

"She also said I would break your heart. As it turns out you broke mine."

She reached out and touched his hand. "I've regretted that many times, but the lure of the big city was too strong. I needed to get away from Rocktown. I felt trapped. I needed more than Rocktown could give."

"Well, you did get that. Look at you, married to one of the richest men in the county, a man with so much money he could buy Rocktown. Do you have any children?"

She sighed. "Allan didn't want any. Not yet, anyway. He always said his business didn't allow him time for kids. They're only a nuisance, anyway, according to him."

"How about you? Don't you miss having children?"

She didn't answer right away. Then she said with a low voice, "I do. I'm thirty. The clock is ticking. The older a woman gets, the better the

65

chances of having a child that isn't normal. I've seen that too many times when older women get pregnant. Nature intended women to have children when they are still young not when they're old."

"You are right, but unfortunately too many people get married now when they are already in their thirties. The long time it takes these days to get a good education and to build a career has a lot to do with that."

"Talking about career," Claire said, "did you ever follow your dream of joining a national team?"

Shaking his head, he said, "I'm a lawyer now. A criminal lawyer, actually."

"Congratulations. I'm sure you have a successful practice. Let's face it, there are plenty of criminals around that need defending. Are you married?"

He nodded. "I am."

"Your wife, is she from Rocktown?"

"No. Her name is Evelyn. She's from Riverhill."

"Happily married?"

"I am." He hesitated. "I was. Evelyn had an accident a couple of years ago. She's in a wheelchair now."

"Oh, I'm so sorry to hear that. I don't know what to say."

He reached for the wine bottle and poured himself a glass. Staring into the dark liquid, he said, "It's been rough. She's paralyzed from the waist down." He paused and looked into his glass. "But that isn't the worst. She's got cancer. The doctors gave her less than a year to live. The way she is right now, she may not even live another month."

"That's terrible. Must be hard on you."

"It is. And on her. I admit I'm going through a difficult time. It isn't easy seeing her lying there, so helpless. She was such an active person before the accident. We were happy, you know. Everything was going so well for both of us. I long to hold her in my arms. We haven't been intimate since her accident." He lifted his glass and put it against his lip but changed his mind and put it back onto the table. "And you? Are you happy in your marriage?"

"To be honest, no. Allan's twin-brother died a couple of years ago and our marriage hasn't been the same since. He barely looks at me now. We haven't had sex for two years." She looked into Roy's eyes. "It seems neither one of us has been lucky with the choices we made. Destiny has dealt us a lousy hand."

"Destiny has nothing to do with it, Claire. We did it ourselves. You should never have left and I should have never let you go." He emptied his glass and lifted the bottle. "I think we need to order another one. This one's empty." He waived to the server and pointed at the bottle. The girl nodded and came back with a full bottle a short time later. She poured wine into Claire's glass.

Roy raised his glass in a toast. "To us and the life we missed. I've been searching for solace in the bottle. It hasn't helped my career or my family life. How are you dealing with it?"

"The sex or the love of a partner?"

"Both."

"I search for it elsewhere."

"Have you found it?"

"Love—no. Sex?" She shrugged.

"Do you have a lover? I mean to satisfy your craving for sex? You've always had a strong sex-drive. I remember when we did it every night. You could never get enough. We weren't even married."

She downcast her eyes, a little embarrassed, as she remembered. "Yes," she said with a smile, "we were two sex-crazed lovers. Maybe it was a good thing we didn't get married. We might have killed each other with passion. All the different positions we tried. Remember when your legs got so weak you couldn't stand and had weak legs for a couple of days?"

He laughed. "I remember. That's the position where we made love standing and I held you like a pendulum in front of me. You were moving your butt in my hands like a woman gone mad. It was quite strenuous for me. I also remember I had a game the next day and it was torture. I didn't perform well that day. You were some kind of hot wildcat in those days."

"Now you are embarrassing me."

"Nothing to be embarrassed about." He looked her in the eyes. "We were crazy about each other. We loved sex and we loved dancing." Glancing at the band playing in the corner, he said, "You wanna dance?"

"I don't know. I haven't danced for years. Allan was never into it."

He rose and held out a hand. "Come on. It'll be fun. Evelyn and I used to dance, but she didn't dance the way you did. She never took dancing lessons and didn't know how to dance the classic dances."

She got up and moved into his arms. It felt a little awkward at first and she stepped on his feet a couple of times. Closing her eyes, she relaxed and concentrated on the gentle sounds of the saxophone. It didn't take her long to feel the rhythm of the music. Roy led her around the dance floor the way she remembered, and it felt good to be in his arms.

She leaned her head against his shoulder and moved with him, forgetting all her problems for a little while.

"I still love you, Claire," he whispered into her ear. "I'm glad you came. I haven't felt his happy for a long time."

She looked at him and smiled. "I'm glad I came, also."

After the third dance, he said, "I believe they just served our food."

"Then we better go and eat. Even though I could dance all night with you."

He smiled. "The evening is young."

They took their seats at the table again. Claire reached for her glass. "Dancing made me thirsty."

"Me, too."

By the time they were done eating, they had emptied the second bottle of wine.

"I need to go to the washroom." Claire rose from her seat. "Oops," she said, as the room began to spin a little. "I believe I drank too much." Her words came out somewhat slurred.

"You can't drive home in this condition, Claire."

She giggled. "I drove here all by my little lonesome. I think I can manage to find my way home again."

"Not a good idea. I won't let you get behind the wheel drunk the way you are." Roy got up, came around and took her arm. "I have a room in this hotel. You'll stay with me until tomorrow morning. You'll be sober then and able to drive home."

She waggled a finger at him. "Are you trying to get me into your bed, Mister Sanders? I'm a married woman, you know."

"And I'm a married man. I'm trying to save you from killing yourself on the freeway. Let's go upstairs."

Even in her tipsy state she didn't miss that Roy was also slurring his words a little. They made it to his room without falling over each other. Roy opened the door and motioned with his hand, "After you, my Lady."

"As always the gentleman," she commented and laughed. She stumbled into the room, kicked off her shoes and flopped onto the bed. He sat on the edge of the bed. There was more than just curiosity in his eyes as he seemed to study her. "Did I tell you that you are even more beautiful than I remembered?"

"No, you didn't." She lifted her arms. "Come and hold me for a little while."

He shrugged out of his jacket and hung it over the back of a chair. Then he took off his shoes and lay down beside her. She looked into the warmth of his brown eyes and the desire for his love was suddenly strong inside her. "Make love to me, Roy. Make me forget my problems and let me make you forget yours. Let's pretend I never left and we are still lovers."

He stroked her hair with a gentle hand. "Yes," he whispered. "Let's pretend we are still lovers."

She put her hand on his chest. "Give me a chance to freshen up first. I really have to pee." She giggled, feeling silly saying it but also comfortable. It was eight years ago. She was back in his room and his parents had gone away for the weekend. They had the whole weekend to make love as often as they wanted. And she wanted it. Needed it.

In the bathroom, she washed her face with cold water and put on fresh lipstick, wasting little time. Inside her, the desire for Roy burned hot, a flame that needed to be extinguished. The alcohol made her forget where she was. Everything seemed right. After taking off her dress and bra, she walked back into the room, wearing only silky panties.

He lay already on the bed, stark naked, sprouting a huge erection.

She laughed. "Still the same I see. You haven't changed a bit."

"Neither have you." He sat up and watched as she came closer. "Those panties have to come off."

"You can take them off with your teeth. Or have you forgotten how to do it?"

"It's been awhile, but I think I can manage." He leered like a teenager who sees a naked girl for the first time.

She climbed onto the bed and stood in front of him. He got onto his knees and licked her belly. Then he grabbed the top of her scanty panties with his teeth and began pulling them down. She laughed and helped him by wiggling her hips. When her panties were far enough down to expose her shaved pussy, he put his tongue into her slit.

71

She moaned and grabbed a handful of his hair. "That feels so good."

He grasped her panties with both hands and pushed them down while licking her pussy lips. She stepped out of her panties and kicked them onto the floor. Then she sank down and stretched out on the bed, her legs wide open. "Put it in already," she moaned. "I'm too horny to wait any longer." She giggled and grabbed his erection. "I can see this big feller is also getting impatient."

He fell between her spread legs. She felt his hard penis at the entrance to her folds and moaned, "Come on, don't dilly-dally, and push it in." She lifted up to give him easier access. When he finally slid into her wetness, she cried out and pushed up against him, jerking her lower body as she tried to take more of him inside her.

They slammed into each other for a long time. She heard a woman sobbing, realized it was her own voice.

"I love you, Claire," he groaned. "I love you so much."

"I love you, too," she whispered, digging her fingers into his tight buttocks. She knew he was on the verge of coming and braced herself.

"I'm ready," he called out hoarsely. "Now…now…His buttocks tightened in her hands and he shuddered between her clutching thighs.

She tightened her inner muscles around his spurting shaft and wrapped her legs around his butt, trying to keep him lodged inside her. His hardness softened and then he slipped out of her. She untangled her legs and relaxed with a deep sigh. He kissed her gently and murmured, "That was wonderful, Claire. Just like old times. You haven't lost it yet. That pussy of yours still fits me like a glove."

She laughed and stroked his hair. "It's still the same pussy."

"Yeah, but I'm sure it wasn't idle these last eight years. I'd sure like to know how many dicks have sampled your sweet honey-pot."

'More than I'd like to remember'. She pulled her eyebrows together. "Why do you want to know? Does it really matter?"

"I'm just curious. You're a beautiful woman and you love sex. An active pussy like yours has to wear out and loosen over the years."

"Where did you hear or read that crap?"

He lifted his shoulders. "I don't know. Probably just guy-talk. We wonder, you know."

"How about your dick? He must have dipped into a score of eager pussies. Did it get smaller from all that friction?"

"Of course not. Neither did it get any bigger, but you may not believe this, there weren't as many women as you might think or as I may have wished for." He laughed. "It was a dumb question. Forget it. It isn't really my business what you did all these years."

"No, it isn't, but to satisfy your curiosity, there weren't as many men to stretch my pussy as you might think. Remember, I've been married four years now, and my husband and I haven't had sex for the last two." No need to tell him about Randy and the other men she'd slept with during those two years. She felt disappointed and let down. He had spoiled a beautiful moment. "You're getting heavy and I'm suddenly quite tired. I want to go and wash up anyway. Maybe take a shower."

"What for? I could lick your body clean with my tongue." He grinned.

"I wouldn't taste very good." She smiled and kissed him on the nose. "It's your fault. You've made me lose control and work too hard. I feel grimy and my skin is slick from perspiring. I need that shower."

"Okay. Go ahead." He moved to his side of the bed and watched her as she slid from the bed. "You still have a beautiful ass and your tits haven't lost their shape," he commented as she walked toward the bathroom.

She turned around and pushed out her chest, thrusting her breasts at him. "I'm only thirty, you know. I hope these will stay like this for many years to come." Then she disappeared into the bathroom.

She looked at her disheveled hair and ran her fingers through it. "You look a mess, girl," she said to her reflection. She had to admit, making love to Roy had been great. It brought back memories of simpler and happier days. His question had hit a sore spot. If her life would have depended on answering his question, she would have had a difficult time answering it.

How many men did she sleep with since that first time when she should have been playing with dolls still? She had lost count. Too many, that was for sure. She never told Roy about the things she did before him. Neither did she tell Allan. When she met Allan, he assumed she was an innocent small-town-girl. She never corrected him. Obviously, he realized she wasn't an untouched virgin the first time they had sex. When he asked her about the guy who took her virginity, she told him she had been engaged for a short time to Roy. They had sex but not often. Only a few times and she never liked it. She only did it because she wanted to please him, foolishly believing she loved him. He was the only man she ever did it with. Allan believed her and never brought it up again.

She smiled at her image. Contrary to what some men believe, a woman's vagina does not lose its elasticity from having too much sex. No man will ever be able to tell how many times a woman had intercourse before him just by having sex with her, unless she told. Something she wasn't prepared to do. Only a foolish woman tells a man the truth about her sexual past.

She stepped into the shower stall, turned on the water and adjusted the taps. The cool spray swept away the remnants of the alcohol and cleared her mind.

When she returned to bed, Roy was asleep. She smiled. 'I guess I exhausted him. I hope he'll be rested in the morning. I'm not leaving until we make love again.'

She slipped under the covers beside him and closed her eyes.

Chapter Five

They did have sex in the morning, but this time it wasn't as out of control as the night before. They took their time, and Claire enjoyed every moment of it. Roy was tender and attentive to her needs. Just like old times. Claire almost forgot that eight years had passed since they had made love for the last time. She pretended she never left. The eight years never happened and it had all been a nightmare. She lay breathing hard in his arms, her eyes closed as she glowed in the aftermath of their lovemaking.

The ringing of her phone reminded her quickly and with cruelty of her real life. It was Allan. "Where the hell are you at this time in the morning? And don't tell me you're shopping. The stores are closed."

Trying to still her breathing, she said, "Of course not. I'm in a hotel. An old girlfriend of mine called me unexpectedly. We had a few drinks and I'm afraid I drank a little too much. I figured it would be best to stay overnight in the hotel. I didn't expect you back for another day and didn't see any harm in not staying home. Is there a problem?"

"My father is turning fifty-five today and he is celebrating it big. I certainly hope you haven't forgotten about that. There'll be important people attending; subcontractors, government officials, CEO's from large companies, and a few investors. Even a couple of movie-moguls. He expects both of us to be there. Make sure you're home on time. Buy a new dress. I want you to make a good impression."

"I suppose you want me to look like a hooker again?"

"Your sarcasm is lost on me. I never said you should dress like a hooker. There is a difference between looking sexy or like a prostitute. Just wear a nice dress that shows off your figure. That's all I ask."

Before she could comment, he cut the connection.

"Prick," she swore and felt like throwing the phone across the room.

"Your husband, I assume?"

She turned around to face Roy. "Yes, that was him. I'm afraid I have to leave. It's his father's birthday today. He's turning fifty-five. I need to be there."

He pulled her back into his arms. "I was hoping you could stay another night. Last night made me feel young again and alive. I haven't been with a woman since Evelyn's accident. I'd almost forgotten how it feels to make love to a woman."

She smiled and stroked his cheek. "And how did it feel?"

"Glorious. The fact that it was with a woman I still love made it even more pleasurable. You and I were good together. Still are. If circumstances were different, I'd ask you to leave your husband and move in with me."

"You know that's impossible."

"I know. I could never leave Evelyn. She needs me now more than ever."

"Do you love her?"

He nodded. "She's a wonderful woman. Beautiful, intelligent, and she has a great sense of humor. Even the accident couldn't take that away from her." He looked at the ceiling. "I feel guilty for cheating on her. As much as I would like to, but we can never do this again, you understand?"

"I understand. The last thing I would want to do is break up your marriage."

"You told me you are in an unhappy marriage. I'm sorry to hear that."

"There is no more love lost between me and Allan. Our marriage is finished. For him, I'm just an inconvenient obstacle in the house, an uninvited guest. He needs me only to make a good impression with his customers. Perfect marriage and stuff like that, you know."

He sighed. "The hardest part for me is having no sex with my wife. Even though she is paralyzed, I'm still attracted to her. How do you handle it?"

She felt like saying, 'I fuck any man who pretends to love me', but instead she smiled and said, "Don't you know the rules? Never ask a woman about her sex-life. You won't get an answer, anyway."

"Well, in a way you've answered my question. Even though it isn't my business how many men you've slept with, I'm still jealous to think other men have held you in their arms and made you writhe under them with the same passion you displayed with me."

"You're right when you say it isn't your business." She sat up and slipped from the bed. "I'd better get ready. I still have to go and shop for a dress before I go home."

"Have at least breakfast with me."

Shaking her head, she said, "I'd better not. I'll grab something in a diner on the way home." She gave him a sad smile. "It was great to see you again, Roy. I enjoyed this night, but as you already stated, this has to be the only time. We mustn't ever get in touch again. It is best this way for both of us."

He didn't hide his disappointment as he looked at her. "I wish things would be different, Claire. You hurt me deeply when you left. I thought my world had come to an end, but I survived. I even found happiness again with another woman, but you were haunting my dreams many a night, especially these past two years. Seeing you again, feeling that luscious body of yours in my arms and tasting your passion has kindled the fire inside me and brought back the ache. It will be difficult to carry one, at least for a little while." He spoke softly and she could hear the anguish in his voice.

"I'm sorry I did that to you, Roy. I really am. I have many regrets and leaving you is one of my greatest regrets, believe me, but what's done is done. We can't turn back the clock. At least you go back to your wife. I have nothing to go back to but misery." She felt her eyes going moist and turned to go into the bathroom.

'Damn you, Allan, why did you have to call and spoil my short moment of happiness.'

Looking at herself in the mirror and seeing her disheveled hair, she wondered if she should take another shower but changed her mind. It would have to wait until she got back home. She washed and put on her makeup.

Roy was up when she came out of the bathroom. He seemed to have regained his composure and gave her a leering grin. "You are surely taking a chance, young lady, coming stark naked out of my bathroom. I guess you didn't know that you've stumbled into the lair of the infamous lecherous Despoiler of Virgins, did you?"

She had to chuckle in spite of the miserable way she felt. They used to play games like that all the time. "It seems I'm safe, great Despoiler, because I'm not a virgin."

"Damn, my luck, but your body looks so delicious. I might just make an exception with you."

She felt sudden tears welling up inside her. Rushing into his arms, she covered his face with kisses. "Oh, Roy, don't torture me like that. I love you, but we can't change the past. Let me go without feeling so guilty."

When she looked into his eyes, she could see the moisture in them. He held her face between his hands. "My love for you will never die, Claire. I will remember you until my final moments, I promise you that. He kissed her gently and released her. "I wish you could stay another night, but even if you could, it would probably be a mistake." He smiled. "Now you'd better get dressed and go before I drag you back to bed."

She touched his cheek in a gentle gesture. "I will always remember you, also, my Love."

She dressed without another word while he watched her silently. Grabbing her purse, she blew him a kiss and walked out of the door.

The tears came when she sat in her car. She let them flow freely. Sometimes a good cry does wonders, even though the tears smeared up her mascara. She felt better after a while and finally left the parking lot. She'd have to stop somewhere to redo her makeup before she went to buy her dress. She hated to be put on such short notice. Buying a new dress should be an enjoyable event not a fucking pain in the butt. Damn you, Allan!

* * *

The Belmont residence stood on a sprawling estate at the edge of the city, featuring its own golf course. A flock of ducks and geese made the artificial lake their home.

As they approached the mansion, Claire noticed a number of cars already parked in the huge parking lot beside the mansion, but Allan drove his car into the attached garage. It was large enough for half a dozen cars and most of the stalls were occupied. Aaron Belmont loved his cars.

Allan scrutinized her again and nodded, apparently satisfied with her appearance. She had found a red formfitting dress that showed off her figure and complimented her blond hair. The plunging neckline revealed more of her breasts as she would have liked, but Allan seemed to approve. She wasn't sure how he would react if he knew she wasn't wearing panties. Either he didn't care how much of her body she displayed to the eyes of other guests or he wanted to boast. Many of his friends were unmarried men that changed their women as often as their suits. Some of the women were either hookers or some young starlet looking to become famous. All of them were beautiful. A few of his friends would be at the party.

They were greeted at the door by Allan's mother. She was the only one in Allan's family Claire liked. At fifty-two, she was still a nice-looking woman. A little heavy in the hips but otherwise she had kept her figure. She could almost have been Claire's mother with her blue eyes and blond hair, which she had tied into a bun on top of her head. It made her appear taller, but in reality, she was Claire's exact height, which was five foot four inches.

"Nice to see you again, Claire." She gave her a hug. "You look wonderful in that dress. I like the color. I used to have one similar to this one." She smiled. "A little too much cleavage, but I guess that's the fashion these days."

"She looks fine, Mother," Allan said, sounding annoyed.

His mother pulled her eyebrows together when she looked at him. "I didn't imply anything else, Son. Everything alright at home?"

"Things couldn't be better."

"That's good. Your father is in his office. Go and say hello to him and don't forget to wish him happy birthday. You know how he gets when you forget to say it."

Allan made an impatient gesture. "Everything upsets him lately. What else is new?"

She looked at Claire. "How can you live with this man? Sometimes I wonder if he was switched at birth or something."

"That joke has a long beard, Mother. I never found it funny," Allan said.

"I know you never did, that's why I say it. Hopefully, someday, you'll have children and you will look at the world in a different way. You will find no matter what you do it will never be appreciated. Don't let me hold you up. Go and talk to your father."

Before Claire followed Allan, she gave his mother another quick hug. The older woman smiled. "I'm glad to have you as a daughter-in-law. Allan couldn't have made a better choice. He needed you to get over Andy's death."

Claire forced herself to return the older woman's smile. "In many ways he still isn't over it."

"I know. It must be difficult for you to deal with that."

"It is, but I cope. I'd better go with Allan." She turned and hurried after him before he disappeared through the door. She wanted to be with him when he met with his father.

Aaron Belmont was at his private bar pouring himself a drink. He turned when Allan and Claire approached. Seeing them, he put his glass back onto the counter and waited for them to come closer.

"Happy Birthday, Dad."

"Thanks, Son. I hear you signed a lucrative deal. Congratulations."

"I was going to surprise you with the news. How did you hear about it?"

His father laughed. "Connections, Son. Connections. In fact, Mister Tanaka is my guest tonight."

"He's here? How do you know him?"

"I've never heard of him before this, but he knows me. Are you forgetting I'm in the construction business? People know me."

"What does he want from you?"

"He told me he has plans to expand his shoe manufacturing business into the US, which means he will need a warehouse to start with. Eventually, he will move some of the manufacturing here. He also knows other companies in Japan that are planning the same thing. This is a huge and profitable opportunity for me."

Allan nodded approvingly. "There may also be spinoff business for me."

"Now you're beginning to think big." The older man reached for his glass and put it to his lips. He looked at Claire over the rim of the glass before he drank from it. Setting it back on the counter again, he said, "You look fabulous, Claire. As usual. It seems you're getting younger each time I see you." He chuckled. "Or maybe it's because I'm getting older. By the way, the dress suits you. Elke used to have a dress like this one. That was years ago, but I still remember her wearing it. I always liked her in it." He opened his arms. "How about a hug for your father-in-law?"

She stepped closer and put her arms around his neck. "Happy Birthday, Aaron." Then she gave him a kiss on the cheek.

He hugged her to him so hard it took her breath away. Her breasts flattened against his chest. Letting go of her, he took her face between his hands and planted a kiss on her mouth. Feeling weird and shocked by this sudden familiarity, she stepped back.

"One of these days you're going to call me 'Dad'. After all, you're like a daughter to me. This was just a show of my affection for you." He grabbed his glass and emptied it.

"Take it easy on the alcohol, Aaron." Allan's mother had come into the room.

"It's my birthday, for heaven's sake, woman. I want to celebrate."

"Remember what Doctor Lawrence said?"

"Yeah, I remember. If I want to give up all the pleasures in life I might as well let them bury me tomorrow. Alcohol is one of the things I still enjoy. One drink a day is good for your health." He poured himself another glass.

"It never stays with one drink," Elke chided him. "I wish you would start listening to Doctor Lawrence. I don't feel like becoming a widow."

He waved it off. "I'm only fifty-five and plan to hang around for a long time. Don't always worry so much."

"But I do."

"I'm fine. I think I'd better join my guests. Don't want them to drink only my expensive liqueur."

"Still the cheapskate," Allan commented.

"Being frugal has nothing to do with being a cheapskate, Son. Once your guests have had a few drinks they'll never notice if you switch to cheaper stuff. No need to waste the good stuff on them." He opened the door and walked through it.

Elke, Allan, and Claire were right behind him. Claire looked around. Many of the guests were familiar faces, but not all of them, especially the women.

85

"Mingle," Allan told her and walked away, leaving her standing alone. She wasn't surprised. This wasn't the first time he did that to her. When one of the serving girls came up to her, she took a glass from the tray. It turned out to be champagne. She emptied the glass and reached for a second one. 'Might as well enjoy myself'.

Somebody started singing 'Happy Birthday to you' and soon most of the guests chimed in. Claire found it ironic, because she was convinced that the majority of them barely knew Aaron Belmont personally, and some probably didn't care to know him.

She was on her fifth glass of champagne when she observed a young man approaching her. "Good evening. You look so forlorn standing here all by yourself. Looking for company?"

Claire smiled, scrutinizing him openly. He was tall, blond and blue-eyed. He could have been handsome had it not been for his overbite. The thin mustache adorning his upper lip made him look a bit old-fashioned. His British accent only added to that impression. Obviously, this guy didn't know who she was. She decided to play along. "Why? Are you offering?"

"What if I am?"

"Well, I may just be inclined to accept your offer. What's your name?"

He made a slight bow. "Charles Belmont at your service."

"Belmont?" she repeated. "Are you related to Mister Belmont?"

"He's my uncle."

"I see. Is this your first time here at the estate?"

"It isn't, but the last time I was in America was ten years ago. I was born and raised in London, England." He chuckled. "My father was sort of considered the black sheep of the family. He and Uncle Aaron never really got along. May I inquire about your name?"

"It's Claire." She laughed and took a sip from her glass. This might just turn out to be fun.

"Just Claire? No last name?"

She laughed again. "Sure. Edwards. Claire Edwards." It was her maiden-name.

He came closer and looked into her eyes. "You're beautiful. It would be a shame to leave you alone with all these boring people. How about you and I finding a quieter place?" She could smell the liqueur on his breath.

"Okay." She leaned forward and brushed his lips with hers. She practically tasted the pheromones exuding from this young stud. The champagne she had consumed had gone to her head and put her into a high state of arousal.

She knew just where to go. Nobody would disturb them in Aaron's office. It was his sanctuary.

They had barely entered the office when he pulled her to him and kissed her passionately. She ran her hand down to his crotch and felt his hardness. When they broke apart, she giggled. "You're a naughty boy, Charles. Is that for me?"

"It is if you want it." His breath was coming fast. He put his hand into the top of her dress and touched her naked breast.

"Careful," she said. "I just bought this dress."

"Why not take it off? I prefer my women naked, anyway," he panted.

"Okay. Give me a hand." She presented her back to him. "Slide down the zipper."

He did and soon her dress pooled around her ankles. She heard him suck in his breath when her buttocks were exposed. Stepping out of the dress, she turned around and looked at him in expectation. She could feel the wetness between her legs seeing the lust in his face.

He let out a low whistle. "You've got a lovely body. You must be one of the models."

She smiled. "Sort of." She pointed to her shaved pussy. "Is this what you want?"

He nodded. She walked up to him, opened his belt and pushed his pants down to his knees. Putting her hand into his briefs, she curled her hand around his hard penis. He moaned and helped her to free his straining member.

She let go of him and walked to the desk, wiggling her buttocks. She smiled when she heard his loud groan. Sitting on the edge of the desk, she opened her thighs. "Come and get it," she crooned.

He crossed the last steps like an eager teenager getting his first glimpse of a woman's sex-organ. Stepping into the inviting space of her spread thighs, he guided his stiff penis between her thick lips and entered her with one mighty thrust.

She cried out softly when she felt his hard organ fill her completely and heard his satisfied grunt. Digging his fingers into her buttocks, he moved in and out of her with erratic movements until she grabbed his hips and steadied him. "Easy, Love," she whispered. "There is no hurry."

"I must confess, I haven't been with many women," he almost stammered. "I don't have much experience."

"That's okay," she moaned. "I have enough for the two of us. How old are you?"

"Just turned twenty." His words came out strained.

"Twenty. Oh my, I'm having sex with a child."

"I consider myself a grown man without sexual experience." He grunted again and stopped moving.

"Don't stop," she moaned.

"I don't want to come yet," he groaned. "This feels so wonderful."

"Whatever you do, don't pull out," she whimpered. "Come inside me. I'm on the pill, if you know what that means."

"I know what it means. I'm not naïve, you know."

"Good." She closed her eyes and concentrated on the hard but pliable object moving inside her hot sheath. Just knowing he was so young was an immense turn-on.

She was at the verge of having another orgasm, when Charles stopped moving and pulled out with a "Bloody hell, who are you?"

Opening her eyes, she stared at a familiar but unwelcome face. "Bakshi," she whispered.

"Hello, Claire. Cheating on your husband with a schoolboy?"

"I'm not a schoolboy," Charles protested.

Bakshi looked down at Charles' still erect penis. "Looking at the size of your dick one might be inclined to believe you." He turned his attention back to Claire. "It seems you like big dicks. Tell

89

you what, let's get rid of this boy and be fucked by a grown man."

"Now listen here, Mister..." Charles grabbed Bakshi's arm.

Bakshi backhanded him across the lips. "Now disappear and let a real man finish what you started. Go before I get violent!"

Charles pulled up his pants and staggered out of the room, covering his mouth with one hand.

Claire watched as Bakshi shoved down his pants and released his penis. He was only half erect but she couldn't help but notice its size. She had trouble formulating a coherent thought; drinking five glasses of champagne in such a short time was finally demanding payment. When Charles pulled out of her, he left her in a high state of arousal and she knew she wanted that big thing inside her.

"It'll be okay, Claire. Don't worry, I'm not going to hurt you, unless you make trouble. Let it happen and we'll both enjoy it. I'm not a rapist."

She nodded, watching his face. It didn't matter what he said. When she was stimulated like this, all rational thoughts left her. She needed to still that terrible hunger inside her at any cost. Deep down she knew, her consumption of alcohol aided in clouding her mind, but she was beyond caring. Closing her eyes, she felt him enter her. He was bigger than Charles, but she was more than primed, and he slid easily into her. A soft cry escaped her lips but not from any pain. She began floating in a sea of pure pleasure and when she opened her eyes, she didn't see Bakshi's face but the face of Roy.

"Roy, my Love," she moaned loudly. "You make me so happy."

She closed her eyes again and when she felt him shudder between her clutching thighs, she sobbed and clawed at the desk. He left her then and she lay back on the desktop, her eyes still closed. After a while, she slipped from the desk and searched for her dress. She dressed, grabbed her purse and stumbled out of the room through a side door, heading for the bathroom. She knew she looked a mess. She also realized that Bakshi practically raped her, but then again, she hadn't struggled. In a way, she gave him consent, anxious even to feel him inside her. That could not be considered rape. He had not hurt her in any way. In fact, he had almost been gentle and given her great pleasure. Her pussy and insides were still tingling in the aftermath. How could she even be upset? Perhaps she misread him and he wasn't such a bad guy after all.

Her reflection in the mirror seemed to disapprove. The image of Bakshi and Salsky holding a third man under water popped into her mind. Then again, was it possible that her imagination had been running wild?

She cleaned herself up and washed her face with cold water. It helped to get her thoughts back in order. After fixing her makeup and hair, she scrutinized herself in the mirror and was certain nobody would suspect what she had been up to.

It seemed she had not been missed. She saw Allan talking with Mister Tanaka, his new client. Bakshi was nowhere to be seen, but she spied Charles Belmont sitting at one of the tables all by himself. Debating if she should join him, she saw no harm in doing it. When she came close, she noticed him nursing a glass of wine and his swollen upper lip.

"Hello Charles," she said "Mind if I join you?"

He looked up at her, trying to smile, but it only turned into a smirk. "If you must."

She sat down and reached across the table to touch his hand. "I'm sorry about what happened."

He pulled back his hand. "You have nasty friends, Claire."

"If it makes you feel any better, he isn't my friend."

"You let him fuck you." His tone was accusing. He sounded hurt.

"I'm sorry about that too. It was out of my control. I wasn't myself. You must believe me."

"Who was that bloke anyway?"

"Nobody important. I don't even like him."

"You sure didn't behave that way. I mean, I didn't see you putting up much of a fight."

"In a way it was your fault."

"What? How can it be my fault?" When a few people standing near them turned their head to look at them, he lowered his voice. "How can you say that?"

She leaned closer and almost spoke in a whisper, "You got me so hot I couldn't think straight. I get like that when I'm horny."

He tried to smile and winced, touching his upper lip. "You're saying I did that?"

She nodded. "You're one great stud, my young English lover."

He sat up straight and grimaced. "Perhaps we can do it again? Possibly, in more private surrounding?"

92

She smiled and shook her head. "I'm afraid we'll have to leave it at this one time." She got up from her chair. "How long are you staying in town?"

"Just a couple of weeks."

"Where are you staying?" She chuckled. "Don't read anything into that. I'm curious."

"I'm staying here with my uncle."

"Then you have a bit of a surprise waiting for you. I'm positive we'll meet again." She blew him a kiss. "See you around, Charles."

She turned around and bumped into another person. "Oh, I'm sorry."

"It's my fault." It was a woman.

Claire realized it was Samantha, Allan's sister. "Hi, Samantha. It's been awhile."

"I know. We were in Europe for a couple of months." She laughed. "You know, we models travel a lot." She looked at Charles. "Hello, Cousin. My father told me you're here. Last time I saw you I did a shoot in London. Three years ago. You haven't changed much. Glad you could make it. I see you've met my sister-in-law Claire."

"Yes, I have. She's charming and beautiful." Charles chuckled uneasily, glancing at Claire. "You never told me you're Saul's sister. You said your last name was Edwards. Does that mean you're married?"

"Her last name is Belmont. She's married to my brother Allan." Samantha gave Claire a startled look. "Why would you lie about that?"

With a pleading look at Charles, Claire said. "Charles told me he loves mysteries, so I gave him one and played the mysterious stranger. I wanted it to be a surprise when he found out he and I were related, or almost related, through marriage that is. He and I aren't really cousins the way he and you are, which means we aren't related. Right, Charles?"

Samantha lifted her hands in an exaggerated display of exasperation. "Now that was a longwinded clarification if I ever heard one. Am I missing something?"

Claire was still staring at Charles, hoping he wouldn't give away their secret.

Charles sat looking like a man who had just been told he was going to be arrested for committing a crime but wasn't sure if he actually committed one. He returned Claire's stare. "What a surprise," he finally said.

Claire forced herself to laugh. "Well, it's out now. I hope there aren't any bad feelings."

Charles came out of his chair and gave Claire a hug. "It was a delight meeting you, Claire." Then he hugged Samantha. "Good to see you again, Cousin Samantha. I hope everything is well with you and your husband?"

"It is. Saul is going to play the leading role in an upcoming movie. They will begin shooting next month."

"That's nice. What's the movie called?"

She almost whispered when she replied. "It's all hush-hush still. All I know it's about spies and the war in the Middle East. It'll be a breakout role for Saul."

"I'm excited for him." Charles gave a little laugh. "Perhaps I should approach Saul and ask him to put in a good word for me for a supporting role. I did some plays in school."

With a shake of her head, Samantha said, "I believe most of the spots have been filled, but I guess it won't hurt to ask."

Charles glanced at Claire. "Do you by any chance have a part in the movie? You're quite a good actress. You would probably be great in love scenes."

She didn't miss his sarcasm but wasn't insulted. "Thanks for the compliment, but I'm not interested in making movies. That's all make-believe. I'd rather experience the real thing." She smiled. "It's more fun, don't you think so?"

"It certainly is, if things go smoothly." He smirked. "I'm afraid I don't have much experience in that department."

"By the way, what happened to your lip?" Samantha inquired.

Charles shrugged. "It's nothing. I had a run-in with a door."

"Looks like the door won." She chuckled.

With a glance at Claire, "Some doors close quicker than expected."

Claire had to admit he had a good sense of humor and didn't seem to carry a grudge. "They do, but there is always a chance they might open again."

"I'm not sure if it would be safe to enter through that door a second time." He grimaced and touched his lip again. "Too many dangers may lurk behind that door."

"I have no idea what you two are talking about," Samantha said. "Anyway, I want to talk to

95

some people I haven't seen awhile. Great to see you, Charles. We'll talk more at dinner tomorrow night. We're planning a barbeque for my father. Just the family." She looked at Claire. "See you tomorrow. By the way, you look nice in that red dress." She smiled. "A bit too revealing for me, but I assume Allan approved." She walked away before Claire could comment.

Claire looked after her and whispered, "Bitch!" She never cared much for Samantha and the feeling was mutual.

She turned back to Charles. "See you tomorrow."

Chapter Six

To Claire's surprise, Allan stayed home in the morning and had breakfast with her. "You look like crap," he said. "Did you have too much to drink last night, again?"

"What else should I have done? You abandoned me, as usual, and left me standing there," she countered. "All by myself."

"You weren't alone. I saw you talking to Charles."

"Yes, we talked, but he's twenty years old. We don't have much in common."

"I'm sure he got a good look at your tits," he sneered. "You did display them freely enough."

"It was your idea."

"When Tanaka was here, but you could have been a bit demure at my father's birthday party."

"Well, you gave me the once-over and you seemed to be satisfied with my appearance."

"I didn't want to make a big scene, but I wasn't happy."

"You weren't happy. When was the last time you were happy with me? You never look at me anymore. You don't seem to care what I wear. You haven't for a long time. Suddenly you do? Are you finally seeing me again?"

"Let's not go there, okay? I don't want to argue. Let's be civil and enjoy our breakfast. Oh, one more thing. Wear a different dress to the barbeque tonight. Can you do that for me?"

"Whatever you want, Allan. It doesn't matter to me."

"Good." He reached for the orange juice and poured it into his glass. "I noticed you had a talk with my sister."

"I did. She told me Saul is going to be a big movie star."

He chuckled. "Saul is a nice guy and I like him, but he'll never be a big star. He's got as much talent as a monkey."

"Samantha said he's starring in a spy action flick. It's still a secret."

"Probably a B-movie, like most of the movies he's been in. Like I said, he's got no talent. I offered him a job in my company, but he said he has to follow his dream." He laughed. "Some people are winners, like me, and some are losers. You can shove them head first into an opportunity, but they are too stupid to take it. That's just the way it is."

"It seems your father is going into business with Tanaka. I hope it works out for him. I don't trust the man. Neither do I trust his lawyer, Mister Bakshi. He's a murderer. But I told you that already."

He gave her an icy stare. "You did. I don't think you have the smarts to advise me or my father on business. I told you the last time to forget what you imagined you saw. I hope you don't entertain any ideas of still going to the police with that crazy talk. There is a lot of money at stake here. Don't screw it up!"

"I know what I saw, but you don't have to worry, I won't interfere in your affairs. Maybe I'm wrong. I hope so, but if I'm not I can say that I warned you and no blame will come to me if things go sour with your and your father's business."

"Duly noted. I'm confident with my decision. In my business, I've learned to become a good judge of a man's character and I have good vibes with Tanaka." He wiped his mouth with a napkin and got up. "I still have some business to take care of. I'll be back by four. I want to leave the house by five. Make sure you're ready."

"I'm always ready in time, but you wouldn't remember that."

"If you say so. Just be ready, that's all I'm saying." He stalked off without looking back.

"Would you like another cup of coffee? It's freshly brewed."

Claire looked up to see the maid standing slightly behind her and wondered if she's been there all along. "Thanks, Carol. I believe I will have another one. Maybe it'll clear my headache."

Carol filled her cup. "Funny you should say that. My boyfriend swears by it." She winked. "Especially a headache from a hangover."

"Your boyfriend is wise." Claire chuckled and regretted it immediately. "From now on I may never touch another drop of wine." She touched her forehead. "I think a bunch of woodpeckers took up residence in my head."

Carol laughed. "My boyfriend calls them guys with jackhammers. He works on construction, you know. Makes good money, too."

"That's important. You love him?"

Carol nodded. "I do. We've been talking marriage. He's saving money to buy a house. Of course, we'll never be able to live in a house like

99

this one. Only really rich people can afford that. You're lucky to be married to Mister Belmont. You can afford to buy anything you want."

Claire looked at Carol. "Yes, I can, but do you really think to be able to buy anything you want is the most important thing in a marriage?"

"I wouldn't say the most important, but it solves a lot of problems."

"It also creates many problems. Let me ask you something. You've been in our employ long enough to see and hear things. From what you observed, do you think Mister Belmont and I have a happy marriage?"

Carol looked away, obviously avoiding looking Claire in the eyes. "It's not my place to judge, Missis Belmont."

"I didn't ask you to judge. Just tell me what you think. I won't hold it against you."

"Well, it seems to me there isn't much love lost between you and Mister Belmont." She stopped and stammered, "I'm sorry, I shouldn't have said that. It's none of my business."

"It's okay, Carol. You only spoke the truth. It wasn't always like that. Love is a precious but fickle thing. It can quickly turn to hate, or at least to indifference. Should you get married to your boyfriend or any other guy, enjoy the euphoria you'll experience in the beginning, but be prepared to eventually come down from that cloud of happiness. It won't hurt so badly when it happens."

Carol stayed silent.

"Don't let me discourage you, girl. Give your man all the love you're capable of and take everything he gives you." She smiled. "Make sure, though, you leave some until you get married. It'll be twice as great. Always remember, it takes two to make it work. Many couples stay in love forever. I wish for it to happen to you. You're a nice girl and deserve the best."

"Thank you, Missis Belmont. I'm sure things will turn around soon for you. I hope so." She reached out to touch Claire's hand but pulled back at the last moment. "Always keep the faith. That's what my mama used to say."

"People who have faith are lucky people indeed. I'm not that lucky. Never been a churchgoer myself." Claire drank from her coffee cup. "Go get me a banana and bring me an aspirin for this friggen headache. Maybe later on you can help me find a suitable dress to wear for tonight's barbeque. I'm sure you heard what my husband said."

"I'll be glad to help you with that." Carol hurried away to get the banana.

In a way, Claire envied her. Still young, looking forward to getting married, buying a modest home, and having children. She'd probably never be rich and live in a ten-million-dollar mansion. She would never have to deal with all those rich bitches that pretended to be her friends. The friends she'd have would be true friends, facing the same mundane problems regular people have to live with on a daily basis.

Of course, there was nothing wrong with being rich, but all the money in the world meant nothing without the love of a husband. No money could warm a cold bed or replace the loving arms of a man.

101

Carol came back with the banana. "Will there be anything else, Missis Belmont?"

Claire shook her head. "I'm fine. Just go about your other chores."

The day seemed to be shaping up nicely. It was already getting warm and it promised to be a hot day, perfect to spend a little time at the pool and maybe do some tanning. She would have liked to talk to Carmen, but she didn't want to call her and interrupt her time with David. Carmen would call when she got home.

She changed into her bathing suit and did a few lapses in the pool. After that, she relaxed on her lounge.

Things would have been perfect had it not been for the boring and loveless life she led. Her thoughts drifted to Roy and she wondered how her life would have been had she never left Rocktown and married him. They probably would have at least a couple of children. Roy always wanted children. He would not have married Evelyn and she may never have been in an accident. It seemed the road she took had affected so many people in a negative way. If she could turn back the clock, she would choose to stay in Rocktown. Strange, how one person has the ability to unknowingly mold people's lives, but do people really have a choice which road to take? What if everything was ordained? Like a play that was already written. Was there a puppet master pulling all the strings?

She sighed. It was useless speculation. What was done was done, but somehow, she couldn't accept the idea that she was nothing more than a puppet. Nobody forced her to leave Rocktown. It had been her idea. She did have a choice in the matter. She could not blame some unknown entity for her actions. It was all on her.

Her headache had slowly subsided, but she knew too many negative thoughts may just bring it back again.

Carol interrupted her contemplation. "Do you want to have lunch on the patio, Missis Belmont?"

She sat up and said, "No, I'll come into the house. It's getting too hot out here. I need to cool down."

"There was a call for you from a Roy Sanders. You were sleeping so I told him you'd call him back. He said it was important. I wrote his number on the pad beside the phone in the kitchen."

"Thank you, Carol." Claire wondered why Roy would call her so soon, especially since they both agreed they should not meet again that way.

He answered on the second ring as if he had been waiting for her call. "Hi, Roy. What's the big emergency?"

"No emergency."

The sound of his voice told her something wasn't right. "What is wrong?"

"Evelyn passed away last night."

"Oh, I'm so sorry, Roy. I feel awful for you. It was...," she hesitated, "...bad timing after, you know. Were you with her?"

"Yes, I was. It happened so fast, around eleven last night. We watched TV when she suddenly said she wasn't feeling well. She turned all pale. I knew something was happening to her. I called the ambulance, but it was too late. She died in my

103

arms." His voice broke. "You know, I did love her, despite her condition."

"I know you did. She was your wife, Roy."

"The funeral will be this coming Saturday. I would really appreciate it if you came."

"I'll try to get away, but I can't promise." She wanted to say 'I love you', but Carol was standing not far away. Instead she said, "You take care of yourself now, Roy." Then she disconnected.

"I'll just have a cup of coffee and a sandwich," she told Carol. "I'm suddenly not very hungry."

"I couldn't help but overhear. Somebody died?" Carol inquired.

"A good friend from my hometown," she said. She never knew Evelyn, but her heart went out to Roy. She wished she could be there to comfort him. A feeling of guilt for what she and Roy had done so close to Evelyn's death rose up inside her. Perhaps it was the universe punishing him for cheating on his wife. What would be her punishment?

She ate her sandwich listlessly and barely tasted the coffee. She hated funerals, nevertheless, she had no choice but to go, hoping Allan had nothing big planned for the weekend.

"Come and help me with the dress," she said to Carol.

When Allan came home, she was dressed and ready to go. The white dress she wore was decorated with pink flowers and green leaves. It covered her chest but was open in the back. A gold rope circled her waist, accentuating her slim figure. He looked at her when he walked through the door.

"Happy with the way I dress?" She gave him a challenging look.

104

"Are you wearing a bra?"

"My breasts are still nice and firm. They don't need support. You would know that if you looked at me once in a while." She put her hands under her breasts and pushed the dress against her body.

"Don't you think this dress is a little bit too flimsy for going braless? I can see your nipples."

"Wearing a bra isn't going to change that. In fact, some bras are designed to show off a woman's nipples."

"You have the answer to everything. I hope you're at least wearing panties."

"They're black and lacy, in case you're interested. Perhaps you want to lift up the hem of my dress and confirm it." She felt annoyed and almost wished he would blow up and start yelling.

He made an impatient gesture with his hand. "You do what you want. Go naked. I don't care. I'm tired and ready to take a shower. This damn heat is making me irritated." He handed his briefcase to Carol and stalked off.

Claire looked at Carol and shrugged. "I guess he doesn't like the dress."

"Do you want to look for another one?"

"Too late for that. I'm wearing this one. We'll be spending time outside on the terrace and I'm not wearing some hot material and sweat to death in this heat."

* * *

Not all the people at the barbeque were family. Claire saw a couple she hadn't seen before. The man was older, but the woman was much

105

younger. They were in deep conversation with Saul Greenberg, Samantha's husband.

Samantha came to greet them when they stepped onto the patio. She nodded to Claire and gave Allan a hug. "How's my big brother these days?"

"Things couldn't be better. I just signed a very lucrative deal. So did Dad. Coincidentally, with the same company." With a glance at Claire, he continued, "Even though some people tell me it's a mistake, but I have confidence in my business skills. Let's face it, I've been in business for many years now and I can spot an opportunity when it comes along."

"I'm happy for you." Samantha laughed. "When it comes to business, I'm a dud. I let my manager handle it for me. So does Saul."

"I hear Saul is going to star in the next blockbuster movie."

Samantha nodded. "You heard correctly. It's all about spies and stuff like that. I can't really tell you more."

"Where is that hunk of a husband of yours?"

"He's busy talking to Jerry Weinstock, one of the directors of his movie."

"I see him. Is that Weinstocks wife? She looks young enough to be his daughter."

"She's just a gold-digger. A wood-be starlet. Nobody important."

"I guess we'd better go and say 'hi' to Dad before he gets annoyed at us. He has such an ego. Come on, Claire."

As they walked past the barbeque, Allan sniffed. "Smells good. How long?"

"Another half an hour or so, sir. A pig needs to be roasted slowly. You can't hurry it," the man at the barbeque said.

"Good. I'm starving."

"We've prepared some delicious appetizers, sir. You and your lovely wife might try those first."

"I might, but I don't think my wife should. She needs to take care of her slim figure." He gave Claire a glance. "Right, honey?"

Claire was about to say 'what do you care about my figure' but bit her tongue and said in her sweetest voice, "I just may make an exception today. I'm slim enough. Don't you think so, honey?"

The man behind the barbeque laughed. "If I may be so bold, you have the slim figure of a gazelle, and eating a few of my appetizers won't hurt you one bit, ma'am."

"Well, thank you. That was the nicest compliment I've heard in a long time. I wish my husband would give me one like that once-in-awhile."

"Don't hold it against your husband, ma'am. Husbands are like that. We take our wives for granted." He sighed. "If my wife had your figure. I'd compliment her every day."

"I'm sure your wife looks just fine," Allan said and pulled on Claire's arm. "Let's move on."

The older Belmont was standing at the edge of the manmade lake with a glass of wine in one hand and smoking a cigar, watching the ducks.

"Hello, Dad," Allan said. "Happy birthday, again."

Aaron turned around. "There you two are. My financially gifted son and my favorite daughter-in-law." He scrutinized Claire. "You look as lovely as ever. That dress does you justice."

It seemed to Claire that his gaze lingered just a little bit too long on her breasts, but it could have been her imagination. Or perhaps wishful thinking. Carmen had suggested she have sex with Allan's father. Somehow, she couldn't help but think it creepy to have sex with her father-in-law. Would that be considered incest?

"You have another daughter-in-law," Claire pointed out.

Aaron blew a smoke ring and watched it expand. "Liz has pulled away from the family. I barely see my grandson anymore. She believes, when Andy died, his share in the company should have passed to her. Of course, she has no leg to stand on. Andy never had a will indicating she should receive his share."

"We've been over that, Dad. Can we drop it?" Allan sounded annoyed.

"I only commented on it because Claire mentioned Liz and I wanted to clear that up, in case there are doubters wondering about what happened."

"There are none, Dad. And if there are it isn't their business."

"No, it isn't. By the way, I have a problem. It could turn out to be huge. Somebody was in my office last night and snooped around in my computer."

"How do you know?" Allan seemed doubtful.

"They left one of the files open."

108

"Don't you password-protect your files?"

"I don't have a password for every file. Who would use my computer but me? I leave my computer on much of the time, but I always close all files. I do it out of habit."

"Which file was it?"

"The open one?" Aaron dropped his cigar and stepped on it, grinding is slowly into the soft grass. "The one that contains a list of my overseas contracts, most them are government contracts. Names, addresses, phone number, contacts. Let's say it contains highly sensitive material."

"Which one of your guests would be interest in that kind of information?" Allan wondered.

"I can think of a few, but I wouldn't want to accuse any of them. Then again, there really isn't one who could or would use the information against me. It wouldn't make sense."

A cold shiver ran down Claire's back. She had a good idea who the intruder was. There was no reason to suspect Charles. He was Aaron's nephew and much too young to be an industrial spy. Aside from the fact that he had been busy screwing her. That left only one suspect.

Mohan Bakshi.

She didn't know when he came into the room. He could have come in only minutes after she and Charles entered the office. All her attention had been on Charles and his big cock and the pleasure he gave her. Of course, Bakshi could have gone back after she left the room to clean herself.

Damn, what a mess! And she couldn't even voice her suspicion. She should have fought the temptation that came over her when Charles told her

109

he was Aaron's nephew and kept her legs closed. The thing with Bakshi would never have happened.

Damn!

"Do you have a camera in your office?" Allan inquired.

"Not in my office. It's the only place where I can sit undistured and unobserved. All the cameras in the house are connected to my computer so I can see what goes on inside and outside the house. No need for a camera in my office."

"You have a camera to capture anyone entering or leaving your office, right? There has to be a record of who did last night."

"You're right, there should be, but there is no record of that. Whoever got into my computer deleted a bunch of pictures."

"How do you know?"

"Because there are no pictures of any of the guests from the first part of the evening. They've been erased."

Claire heaved a sigh of relief. She had completely forgotten about the security cameras in the house.

"Sounds like a professional hit to me," Allan speculated. "You should go to the police."

"And tell them what? I have no proof to back up my claim. I'll bet there are no fingerprints. Whoever did this, knew what he was doing."

"Maybe it was a she?" Allan suggested.

"It's all speculation now. We'll just have to wait and see what happens."

"What do you expect?"

110

"I don't know. I hope nothing will come of it." He looked toward the barbeque. "How is the roasting pig coming along?"

"The guy told us about another half hour. What do you think about Saul's next movie? It's supposed to be some kind of spy action flick."

Aaron chuckled softly. "I hope it won't be a flop like his last one. It's a good thing Samantha is bringing in the money. They'd both be on welfare it they had to depend on his income. Just between us, I don't believe he has any talent. The only thing he's got going for him is his good looks. He would make a better model than movie star. Don't tell him I said that."

Allan laughed. "I believe you and I are on the same wavelength, as usual. Let's go and have a drink together. We haven't celebrated our new ventures yet. I have a good feeling about it."

"So do I." Aaron patted his son on the back. "If we weren't filthy rich already, I'd say we're going to be rich."

Both of them broke into loud laughter.

Claire watched them walk away. She stood alone, feeling neglected and forgotten. When she saw Charles sitting at a table, also alone, she felt pity for the young man and walked over to talk to him.

He looked up when she approached and gave her a crooked smile.

"Need company?"

He indicated one of the empty chairs. "As long as you're not trying to seduce me again."

She took the chair and chuckled softly. "Didn't you enjoy it?"

"Too much, but it didn't end well. What we did was wrong."

"I apologize for not introducing myself properly, but I thought it might be fun. It certainly was a titillating experience. By the way, we did nothing wrong. You and I are not blood relatives."

"But you're a married woman. What's worse, you're married to my cousin. I can't even look him in the eye without feeling guilty."

"Don't feel guilty. Allan and I, we are not a happily married couple."

"If you don't mind me asking, what is wrong with your marriage?"

"Everything. It all started with the death of Andy. It changed Allan. He can't seem to accept that his brother is dead." She lowered her voice. "If it makes you feel any better, we haven't had sex ever since. Perhaps you can understand my frustration. I'm a healthy woman with an appetite for sex."

"I see." He nodded, evidently sympathetic with her predicament. "But that doesn't mean you and I will have sex again. It doesn't feel right."

She smiled. "You're a peculiar young man. Most guys would not hesitate to jump into the sack with me. I'm good at it. Perhaps too good and I like it too much." She sighed. "It's a curse, you know."

"Some people might call you a nymphomaniac." He lifted a hand. "I didn't mean to offend you. My apologies."

"Accepted. You may just be right. By the way, somebody got into your uncle's computer last night. They downloaded some sensitive stuff. I know it wasn't me."

112

He cocked his head. "I hope you're not suggesting I did that."

"Of course not. What would you have to gain from spying on your own uncle? I suspect it was Bakshi."

"Bakshi?"

"The guy who replaced you between my legs." She noticed a sudden color creeping into his cheeks and chuckled. "Am I embarrassing you?"

"In a way. You Americans have a strange way of talking when it comes to sex. Too much detail sometimes."

"Sorry. I forgot you're British. Is everyone in your country so uptight?"

He shrugged. "I don't know. I, at least, don't care much for vulgar talk. I prefer more subtle words."

"You're a sophisticated guy. Nothing wrong with that. You want to hear vulgar talk? Then you should meet my girlfriend, Carmen. Sometimes she even embarrasses me, and I'm not a stuffy old maid. Hey, maybe I should hook you up with her. She loves to screw young studs like you. You wouldn't have to feel guilty. There is no chance you two are related, and she isn't married."

"Thank you, but I believe I'll pass on that one." He looked past her. "Aunt Elke is coming to our table."

Claire turned her head and saw Allan's mother heading for them. "Hi Claire. Hello Charles. We're starting to serve the food. Apparently, the pig is done. You two don't even have anything to drink. Go and get yourself something."

"I'm not much of a drinker," Charles said, "but thank you, Aunt Elke. Perhaps I can get a glass of Apple juice?"

"Well, of course. Just ask Maggie to get you one." Elke walked away.

Charles glanced at Claire. "Who's Maggie?"

"The girl walking around carrying a tray with glasses," Claire explained. "By the way, last night you consumed alcohol. Why not tonight?"

"I can't drink much. It goes to my head fast and I may do things I'll regret in the morning. Like what happened yesterday."

"Oh, Charles, don't lose sleep over it. It happened. Leave it be. Come, I need a glass of wine, anyway. Have you ever tasted barbequed pork? I mean from a whole roasted pig?"

"I have. Hog Roast is very popular in the UK. Americans are not the only ones to roast a whole hog."

"You're right. Sometimes, we Americans think nobody else does the things we do. Here comes Maggie." Claire took one of the glasses filled with wine and said, "Can you get a glass of apple juice for my friend, please."

"Sure. As soon as I get rid of these glasses."

Charles touched Claire gingerly on the arm. "Thank you, Claire. Listen, do you mind if I go and talk to Samantha for a bit?"

"No, not at all. I don't want to keep you all to myself." She smiled and watched him walk away. 'Twenty years old and still a little naïve. Not like me when I was his age. I lost my virginity and my innocence long before that. I wonder if he has a

114

girlfriend back home. He never told me what he does for a living.'

Her thoughts drifted to the previous night. Charles actually came on to her, acting like a man who knew his way around women. As it turned out, it was the alcohol that made him lose his inhibitions. A shame their sexual encounter ended the way it did, and she wondered if he resented her in some way because he didn't reach his climax with her. He left her, his pride hurt and his lust for her unfulfilled. Too bad, she wouldn't get a chance to make it up to him.

Chapter Seven

Carmen called a couple of days later.

"How was the weekend?" Claire didn't really have to ask. How could Carmen not have had a great time with David?

"It was wonderful. We spent most of the time in bed. I just got home last night." She giggled. "An extended weekend. I don't know what got into David. He's usually in such a hurry to get inside me, but he was so different in his lovemaking. He took his time and made sure I was ready for him. The best sex I've had in a long time. The days went by much too fast. I could have stayed with him another week." She giggled again. "I don't know if I would have lasted, though. He sure tuckered me out."

"I'm happy for you, Carmen."

"What about you? Anything exciting happened while I was gone?"

"Let's put it this way—I wasn't bored. Allan and I went to his father's place to celebrate his birthday. He turned fifty-five. That's where I had sex with Allan's twenty-year-old cousin from England."

"What?"

Claire laughed at Carmen's reaction. "Don't sound so shocked. It just happened. He may have been only twenty, but he was, how should I put it, well hung?"

"I get the picture, girl. But, come on, twenty? He's just a kid. You can do better."

116

"I did. Roy called me on Sunday. He asked me to meet him."

"Roy? Isn't that the guy you were engaged to in Rocktown?"

"That's him."

"Did you go?"

"Yes, I did."

"What happened?"

"We had sex."

There was a pause on the other end. After a while Carmen said, "It sounds like you had a busy week. I'm not sure if I should say I'm pleased about your activity. A twenty-year-old almost relative and an old boyfriend?"

"Ex-fiancé," Claire corrected her.

"Okay, ex-fiancé. It doesn't matter. Is he still single?"

"Well, he is now. He was married until a few days ago. His wife passed away last Monday."

"Wow! He couldn't have loved her very much if he had sex with you the day before she died."

Claire sighed. "I know this whole thing sounds awful. She was sick for a long time, but he loved her until the end. She was alive when we saw each other. She died suddenly. Neither of us planned to have sex. He was in town and wanted to talk to me. You know, catch up with our lives. We had dinner, danced a little and one thing led to another. We both drank too much and I ended up in his hotel room. I'm not sorry and I make no apologies."

"You owe me no apology, Claire. You're an adult and you happen to live in an unhappy marriage, but remember, we had a plan? Instead of having sex with that young stud, you should have

117

screwed Allan's father. That would have made more sense. You want to make sure you have a secure future."

"I don't really see how having sex with Allan's father is going to secure my future."

Carmen chuckled into the phone. "I can see you don't have a scheming mind. Take it from an experienced more mature woman. By screwing your father-in-law, you won't have to worry about him advising his son to kick you out. He'll want you around, but he will want to keep your affair with him secret and he'll make sure you keep your mouth shut by making you happy, which means money. Get it?"

"I get it. We'll see. By the way, I'm glad you called. I want to go to Evelyn's funeral and I'd like you to come with me. The funeral is Saturday, but we'll have to fly to Rocktown tomorrow. Please, say yes. I would feel so much better if I had a friend beside me."

Carmen seemed to hesitate, but then she said, "Okay. I'll come with you."

When Allan came home that evening, Claire told him about her plan. "She's an old girlfriend from my hometown and I want to be there. I'm taking Carmen with me."

"Does Carmen know her, too?"

"No, but she's my best friend. That's what friends do when they go through difficult times."

"Well, then I guess we're not best friends, because I'm not coming with you."

"I never asked and I didn't expect it. Has your father made any progress in his investigation to find out who broke into his computer?"

118

"Nothing so far. The investigators told him not to worry about it unless somebody takes some kind of action against him. So now he's just playing a waiting game."

"Is your cousin Charles still here?"

"Why do you ask?"

She shrugged. "Just curious. He seems a bit nerdy."

"I wouldn't know. I haven't really talked much with him. I don't have time for chit-chat with relatives. My father and Uncle Mason never got along, anyway, and I was never interested. I don't know anything about my uncle and Cousin Charles."

"Sometimes it doesn't hurt to be interested in the relatives. You never know when you need them."

"I don't need any relatives. They are like leeches when they become aware that you're a successful businessman with money. Friends can be like that, also. I have no use for them."

"Not all friends are after your money, Allan, but you wouldn't know that, because you don't have any true friends. Did it ever occur to you that your so-called friends may also be nothing but leeches?"

"All my friends are rich. There are no leeches among them."

"They are acquaintances not friends. There is a huge difference. Acquaintances drop you like a hot stone when you fall into difficult times. Friends will stay with you, no matter what."

Allan gave her a sarcastic laugh. "You think you know everything, Claire. If you were as smart as you always pretend to be, you'd be a successful career-woman instead of loafing around the pool all day long or go riding that stupid horse of yours. The wives of some of my friends have their own business or are CEO's of big companies. If you were like them, you would have the right to give advice. The way things are, perhaps you should keep it to yourself instead of pretending you know what you're talking about."

Claire glared at him, anger welling up inside her. "Thank you for those kind words, Allan. You certainly know how to make a woman feel special."

"You're welcome. And now I'd appreciate it if you let me eat my supper in peace without your wise words."

"Fuck you, too, Allan." She got up and stalked away, determined not to let him get under her skin. When she stepped onto the patio, she took a few deep breaths, trying to calm down. She knew she couldn't go on much longer like this. Something needed to happen. Staring at the bright moon, she wished she could climb into a spaceship and leave the whole damned planet behind, but that was only wishful thinking, a fantasy.

Looking at the stars brought her a measure of peace. When she was young, her father had taught her the names of the constellations. She remembered a few but not all of them. She also remembered asking her dad if there were people living on those specks of light. He had laughed and said, "Nobody knows. Some of those specks of light are suns like ours with perhaps a few planets like Earth. They may have intelligent beings living on them, but I doubt they look like us. Some of those beautiful flickering lights are whole galaxies with millions of suns and planets. The universe is wonderful and awe-inspiring. We will never understand it, never get the answers to our questions, but we can dream and speculate."

She sighed, wishing she were that little starry-eyed girl again, with no problems but many questions about the world around her. It could be a beautiful world but also an ugly one.

This was the ugly side of it. Would she ever find the beautiful side?

* * *

She and Carmen boarded the commuter plane shortly before noon the next day. They landed in Denver an hour later. From Denver they took a taxi to Rocktown.

"Nice little town," Carmen remarked, looking at the colorful houses and manicured front lawns as the taxi drove down the main street. "A little too quaint for my tastes, though. I prefer big cities."

"I grew up here," Claire said. "This is my hometown and I've been missing it. Eight years is a long time to be away. Besides, it isn't that small. When I left, more than nine thousand people called Rocktown home. There may be more now. We have everything you find in a large city, only smaller. And Denver isn't that far away."

"I guess I'm just a big-city gal." Carmen chuckled softly. "If I had to choose between Rocktown and Denver I'd prefer Denver."

They booked a room in the Marigold Inn, not one of the swankiest places in Rocktown, but the only one with an available room. Rocktown was a popular tourist attraction and the hotels and motels sold out quickly.

Claire tried to phone Roy, but she only got his voice mail. "Hi Roy. This is Claire. We've arrived in Rocktown. We're staying at the Marigold. My friend Carmen is here with me. This is my cell phone number in case you misplaced it. Call me."

"He's expecting you, isn't he?"

Claire gave Carmen a surprised look. "Of course he's expecting me. I told him I was coming to the funeral. I just didn't tell him I wouldn't be alone."

"Were you afraid something might happen between the two of you?"

"Don't be absurd, Carmen. He just lost his wife. The last thing on his mind would be sex right now."

Carmen shrugged. "You haven't lost anyone and it looks to me you still love him. You may just get this idea that you have to console him. There is no better way to console a man but to have sex with him. I'm your conscience to keep you from doing that."

"Maybe you're right, I don't know. I wanted you to come along as my friend and to keep me company. Isn't that reason enough?"

"Well, I'm here, my friend. I'm hungry. What do you want to do about supper? I noticed they have a restaurant downstairs."

"I've never had supper here and I can't vouch for the food, but I know a nice little place not far away. It's cozy and the food is good. At least it was eight years ago. We'll go there."

"Okay. I'm game."

The place hadn't changed much in eight years. Even the bartender was still the same moonfaced guy with the dour face. Except he had lost the little bit of hair that had seemed glued to his round skull, and he looked older. Now he was completely bald and his cauliflower-ears were even more prominent. A thin mustache adorned his upper lip. Also new since Claire saw him last.

"Hi, Rupert. Still wiping that counter top with the same cloth?"

The man gave her a puzzled look. It was obvious he didn't recognize her. "I change it every day. What are you? The health department?"

Claire chuckled. "Why? Are you scared the place may not pass inspection? You don't have to worry. I'm Claire Edwards. I used to come here often." She sighed. "I was gone for eight years."

"Gone? You mean jail?"

"No," she said with a laugh. "I moved away, to the big city."

"Why?"

She shrugged. "Many reasons. Not all of them valid. Anyway, this is my friend Carmen." She pointed at Carmen.

"What made you come back?" Rupert never stopped wiping.

"A funeral. One of my friends lost his wife. You may remember him. His name is Roy Sanders."

Rupert nodded. "I know him. He still comes here. For a while, he was accompanied by a pretty redheaded woman. I assume it was his wife, but these last couple of years he came alone. Before the redhead, he used to come in with this wild, hot

123

blond chick." He peered at her with narrow eyes. "Now I recognize you. That was you. Sorry, I shouldn't have said it like that." His lips actually moved to form the parody of a smile. "I don't mind admitting I was one of the guys ogling you, wondering how it would be…" He didn't finish the sentence, but Claire didn't have to guess what he meant.

"That was eight years ago, Rupert. I'm not that person anymore."

"You still look hot to me." He gave her a calculating look. "Any chance you and me, you know?"

She shook her head. "It won't happen. I'm a married woman now."

He heaved a loud sigh. "One can dream and hope. Can't blame me for that. Guys like me never get the chance with a woman like you anyway." He looked at Carmen. "How about you? Can I buy you a drink?"

"You can buy me a drink, big guy, but don't expect anything." Carmen gave him a playful smile. "Of course, there is always the chance I might change my mind."

"What would change your mind?"

Carmen laughed, shrugged. Then she leaned across the counter and fleetingly touched his nose with her finger. "You'll have to find that out, my horny friend."

Rupert looked at Claire. "I like the way your friend talks. It's a turn-on, but I think she's just teasing me. Is she serious?"

It was Claire's turn to laugh. "With Carmen one never knows. With her it's a game. If you play the game right you may get lucky—or not."

Rupert shook his head and threw up his hands. "Women! Always playing games."

Claire smiled. "So are men. You're playing your own game, Rupert, except, you're not that subtle about it."

"I'm subtle," he protested.

"As subtle as a horny bull spotting a cow in heat. You may not remember, but you used to hit on me with "Hey, babe, how about you and me going into the room in the back?""

"We never did, did we?"

"I'd remember." She chuckled. "Don't feel bad. Give us a couple of beers and we'll go sit at that table over there. We came to have supper not sex. I hope you're offering something good tonight."

"The food's always good here." He smirked. "The sex, too."

"You're funny, Rupert. You missed your calling. Should have become a comedian." She took one bottle, while Carmen got the other one.

"Some guys honestly believe women were born to satisfy their sexual desires," Carmen said as they headed for their table. "I hope not all men are like him in this town."

Claire slid onto the bench and laughed softly. "Rupert is one of a kind. I'm not saying there aren't others like him in Rocktown, but so far I've only met one—Rupert."

"Thank god for that." Carmen lifted her bottle. "To Rupert. May he find a woman as unique as he."

"By the way, his last name is Sexsmith."

Carmen almost choked on her beer. "That explains everything. It seems he's trying to live up to his name. How old is he anyway?"

Claire shrugged. "Probably in his late thirties." She looked up when the serving girl came to their table. "Bring us your special, whatever it is." She glanced at Carmen. "Is that okay with you?"

"Sure. As long as it doesn't take too long. I'm starved."

Claire looked after the girl as she hurried away with their order. "Sometimes I envy girls like her. I hope her love life is simpler than mine."

"It can be as simple as you make it, girlfriend. By the way, you never really told me how your father-in-law's birthday party went, except that you had sex with Allan's cousin from England"

"I did, but I kept from you that I also screwed Mohan Bakshi." She said it casually, wondering how Carmen would react.

Carmen stared at her. "I hope you were only kidding. You aren't talking about the same guy we saw with that cop drowning another guy by the lake?"

"I'm afraid I'm talking about that same guy. Actually, it was quite satisfying."

Carmen shook her head, obviously confused. "I don't think I understand. Why would you do that? What was he doing at the birthday party?"

"He's the lawyer of one of Allan's and his father's business partners. I'm not going into details how it happened, but he's not such a bad guy. Maybe I misjudged him."

126

"This isn't going the way I envisioned it. You're getting yourself deeper and deeper into a spider's net from which you won't be able to escape. I still say, the only way for you to protect yourself and your future is to have sex with your father-in-law. It will remove the danger of anyone telling him stuff about you. Even if they do, he won't care. There will be nothing he can do to hurt you without putting himself in danger."

"You may be right, Carmen, but it is easier said than done."

* * *

Claire was surprised to see so many people at the funeral service, but perhaps it only seemed so, because the church was not large. She didn't approach Roy until everyone gathered for the reception in the church hall and had offered their condolences. She gave him a brief hug but didn't say anything. Then she introduced Carmen as 'my best friend'.

Carmen shook his hand with the words, "I'm sorry for your loss."

"Thank you for your kind words. As much as it hurts, it is in a way a blessing. She's finally released from her pain." He looked at Claire. "I'm glad you came. Where are you staying?"

"At the Marigold Inn."

He managed a little smile. "Not the ritziest place."

"It's good enough. Besides, it's all we could get at such short notice."

"How long will you be in town?"

127

"A couple of days, maybe."

"Call me tomorrow. Perhaps we can get together for lunch."

"I'd like that." She squeezed his hand and turned to walk away, but he held onto her hand.

"I'm sorry for the way things turned out," he said with a low voice. "I wish your visit here would be for a different reason."

"So do I, but we have no control over what Lady Fate plans for us." She felt sudden tears blurring her vision. "Sometimes she gives us a choice, but most of the time we make the wrong one. I made mine years ago and for that I'm sorry. If I could undo it, I would." She dabbed her eyes with one finger and gave him a brave smile. "Don't let me keep you from your other guests. A few are already looking. Carmen and I will sample some of the dainties. They look good."

As they walked away from Roy, Carmen whispered, "You must have been crazy to let a hunk like that get away. He's not only good-looking, he also seems nice and smart."

"He's a lawyer." Claire chuckled. "He has to have some smarts." She reached for a couple of those tiny sandwiches they serve at funerals. She wasn't really hungry. One doesn't go to a funeral for the food. Looking around the room, she wondered if there'd be anyone she knew or recognized. Many guests would be from Evelyn's hometown. Friends and relatives Claire wouldn't know anyway.

When someone touched her on the shoulder, she turned around to look at the woman standing beside her. She looked familiar, but she couldn't place her.

"I thought I recognized you. Aren't you Claire Edwards?"

She nodded. "I used to be. Now I'm Claire Belmont."

"I'm Sylvia. Before I got married, my last name was Edison."

Something clicked in Claire and she suddenly remembered. She wished she hadn't. "Sylvia. I remember. You used to be blond." She didn't say 'and slimmer'.

"My husband had a thing for redheads. I changed my hair color. Now I'm so used to it." Sylvia laughed. "We had some good times together, you and I." She glanced at Carmen. "You're her girlfriend?"

Carmen nodded.

"My best girlfriend," Claire said. "Her name is Carmen."

"Hi Carmen. Claire and I used to be best girlfriends. It seems ages ago now." She dropped her voice to a whisper. "I don't know if and what Claire told you about those days in our past, but we were a wild bunch. Claire was a pistol if you know what I mean. Even I couldn't keep up with her. We made a ton of money with those horny old guys. Claire and I used to work together. One night we took on five men..."

"Like you said that was ages ago," Claire interrupted. "We were different then. I'm trying to forget those days. So if you don't mind..."

Sylvia shrugged. "Okay, but you have to admit we had fun, and the money we raked in allowed us a lifestyle not many girls like us enjoyed."

"Yes, it did, but can we drop that subject now? I came to console Roy. He just buried his wife."

"I understand. By the way, everyone was surprised when they heard you left Rocktown. We all figured you and Roy would tie the knot. What happened?"

Claire shrugged. "Life happened, that's what. What about you? You indicated you're married."

"I was. For nearly seven years. Divorced now."

"Sorry to hear that. Got kids?"

"Two girls. Six and four. My ex-husband's name is Bill Preston. He owns Preston's Sporting Goods. Inherited the place from his dad."

"Are you living in town?"

"No. I live in Riverhill. Evelyn's parents are my neighbors. That's how I knew Evelyn."

Claire nodded. "I see. Well, it's great to bump into you, Sylvia."

"What about you? You're married I assume? Children?"

"Married, yes. Children, no."

"You don't know what you're missing. You're not a real family until you have children. What does your husband do?"

"He's in advertising." Claire didn't feel like going into her personal life. Sure, she and Sylvia had been good friends, but now they were strangers. They had nothing in common anymore. "Like I said, it was good to see you again. Maybe we can get together sometime, but Carmen and I have to leave now. I promised my parents to visit them tonight. Tomorrow, my brother is coming by, and I want to see him."

"When will you be flying back home?"

"Day after tomorrow."

"Too bad. It would have been nice to get together. Well, take care." Sylvia turned and walked away.

"One would think you'd be happy to see an old girlfriend."

Claire glanced at Carmen. "Normally I would be, but Sylvia was never my best girlfriend as she claims. She was a little bitch. One of the old geezers got her pregnant and she blamed me for it. I was supposed to meet with him that night, but I had made other arrangements and she went instead. It wasn't my fault she didn't take her birth control pills."

"Did she have the baby?"

"No. The guy who got her pregnant paid for the abortion. She left our little club after that. She suggested I share part of my earnings with her because she was out of action. I didn't." Claire shrugged. "I'd rather not talk about it. Those are not my best memories."

They left without saying goodbye to Roy. Claire thought it would be best that way.

"I assumed we wouldn't visit your parents until tomorrow. Change of plans?"

"No change of plans. I didn't feel like getting together with Sylvia. It's Saturday night and I have the urge to go out for a nice and expensive supper. There is a restaurant I would like to visit. I could never afford to have supper there when I lived in Rocktown."

"Sounds good to me."

Chapter Eight

Claire's parents were over-enjoyed to see her.

Her mother cried and even her father had tears in his eyes. He took Claire's face between his hands and looked at her. "You look the same and yet— you have changed. Your eyes. The brightness that sparkled in them is gone. Your eyes look old. What have they seen, sweetheart? What kept you away from your home and us for eight years?"

Looking into his old, wrinkled face made her break out in tears. She flung her arms around his frail body and clung to him, sobbing. "I'm so sorry, Dad. I'm sorry for hurting your and Mom's feelings. I'm sorry for not coming back. I just couldn't bring myself to do it. Don't ask me why."

"At least you did call us the odd time, but even that took two years before you did. We had no idea what happened to you those first years. Didn't even know if you were still alive."

"I'm sorry about that, too, Mom. If I could, I would take it all back."

"You can't. What is done is done, but no sense to dwell on the past. At least, you're here now. Let's not stand in the doorway. Come in and make yourself at home." She glanced at Carmen. "You haven't introduced us to your friend."

"I'm Carmen Garcia. Claire and I are good friends."

Claire's mother held out her hand. "Pleased to make your acquaintance, Carmen. Welcome to our home."

"Thank you, Missis Edwards."

"Don't call me that. Makes me feel old. I'm Grace to all my friends. Go and sit down. I'll make some coffee. You drink coffee, don't you?"

Carmen nodded. "Sure do. Only one cream, please."

Grace hurried away into the kitchen. Claire and Carmen walked into the Livingroom. It was like walking back in time. The furniture was still the same. It wouldn't have surprised her if the plant on the planter by the window was the same plant her mother had nurtured eight years ago.

"This is quaint," Carmen commented.

Claire smiled. "The furniture should have been replaced years ago. My parents are quite old fashioned. They don't even own a computer or a cell phone."

"Nothing wrong with that. Young people are too addicted to their gadgets. I must admit, I'm one of them." Carmen sank into one of the leather chairs. "This feels nice. Everything looks so comfortable."

"I'm surprised to hear you say that. You of all people with your ultra-modern décor should feel out-of-place in surroundings like this."

"I don't. I'll have you know that I adapt to my surroundings. I'm like a chameleon."

"How long could you live among these surroundings before you go crazy? A week? A month? I know you, Carmen. You said yourself you're a big-city girl. You wouldn't be happy living in a place like Rocktown, never mind in an old house with old-fashioned furniture. You can't even live without your cell phone for a day."

Before Carmen could answer, Claire's mother came in carrying a tray with three cups. She handed one to Carmen with 'one cream' and the other one to Claire. "I hope you still like your coffee black with no sugar."

"I do, Mom. Some things never change."

Her mother took a seat on the couch and took a sip from her cup. "Now, fill me in what you've been up to for these last eight years."

Claire gave her a sad smile. "It would take more than an afternoon, Mom. Besides, it isn't as interesting as you might think. Pretty boring stuff living in a big city. Where is Dad?"

"He took a drive to the store. He'll be back shortly."

"It's Sunday. Are you open Sunday's now?"

Her mother smiled. "No. We still believe Sunday's are for worshipping not selling stuff. I hope you haven't forgotten everything we taught you about that. You still go to church?"

Claire shook her head. "I haven't had much urgency to go. Sorry, Mom."

"Your dad and I were afraid that might happen. Religion doesn't seem so important anymore with young people these days. No wonder all these bad things are happening all over the world. People have no respect for God, for the law and for old traditions. It's a shame."

"That's the world, Mom. Not much we can do about it. Religion is overrated."

"It makes me sad to hear you talk like that, Claire. You sound like a person with no hope. Is that what the big city did to you?"

135

"It's a sign of the times. I'd rather not go there if you don't mind. How's Marliese doing? I haven't heard from her for a long time."

"She's doing okay. I just spoke to her a couple of weeks ago. She's got a promotion. I don't know what exactly she's doing, but from what I understand she is one of the senior editors on that newspaper. Means more money, too."

"Money isn't everything, Mom. She's still single, I suppose?"

Her mother made a motion with her hand. "Your sister is married to her job. No time for a man."

"Maybe that's not so bad." Claire sighed. "I miss her. Perhaps one of these days I'll fly to New York and visit her."

When her cell suddenly came to live, she was reluctant to answer it, fearing it might be Allan trying to ruin her day, but it was Roy. "Hi Claire. I was hoping we could get together for lunch."

She got up and walked into the kitchen. "I'm sorry. It's not going to work out. I'm at my parents' place. I can't just leave. Robert is coming tonight. He came in from Denver just to see me. Last time we saw each other he was seventeen. A boy. He'd be so disappointed, as would I."

"Too bad. I was looking forward to seeing you." He hesitated. "Don't take this the wrong way, but I don't want to lose you as a friend. Let's stay in touch, okay?"

She stayed silent for a moment, trying to swallow a lump that wouldn't stay down. Hearing the sadness in his voice and sensing his desperation, she felt like telling him how much she still loved

136

him and how much she missed him. She didn't, knowing it would not be right. She was still married to Allan, and she couldn't give Roy hope there might be a future for them together. She was doomed to spend the rest of her life in a loveless marriage with no way of getting out. Allan would never give her a divorce.

"Claire, are you still there?"

"Yes, I am, Roy. I'll call you once I'm back home and we can talk undisturbed. I don't want to lose our friendship, either. It will be good to talk to a true friend once-in-awhile. I think we both need that, but not today. Take time to mourn your wife and get your thoughts together. Things will get better." She felt moisture on her cheek. 'For you and for me, my Love'. "Bye, Roy. You take care of yourself now."

She cut the connection before he could answer and stared at her shaking hands. 'Why does life have to be so cruel? Why did I ever leave Rocktown and him? We both would be happy now.'

She headed for the bathroom to wipe her face and check her makeup. She didn't want anyone to see her like this. It was her own private hell and nobody could help her.

* * *

"Do you feel like driving out to the ranch this week to take the horses for a ride?" Carmen gave Claire an expectant look.

"Might not be a bad idea. I'll call you." Claire planted a kiss on Carmen's cheek. "Thanks for coming with me. It made things a lot easier."

137

"I didn't mind. You know I'll always be here for you."

"I know." Claire watched the taxi pull away before she climbed into the one waiting for her. She wasn't looking forward to going home.

Allan was standing in the kitchen when she walked in. He turned. "I didn't expect you home yet. I gave Carol the day off. I'm on my way to a meeting and won't be home much before midnight."

She shrugged. "I guess I don't have to give you permission."

"Very funny," he said with a shake of his head. "One would think you'd be in a more somber mood after having gone to a funeral."

"It wasn't meant to be funny. It's called sarcasm."

"Whatever. I don't care." He tilted his head to listen. "I believe my ride is here." He bent to pick up his briefcase. "Don't wait up." With that he walked out of the door.

"I wouldn't dream of it," she said to the closing door. Opening the fridge, she stared into it. 'I should have had lunch at the airport with Carmen. I think I'll fry up a couple of eggs. I'm not really hungry'.

After lunch, she decided to lounge around by the pool. A swim might just lift her mood. Since it was warm outside, she didn't bother putting on her bathing suit. Naked, she padded across the warm tiles and dove into the pool.

After a few laps she felt much better. As she climbed up the ladder she heard a noise. Looking toward the house, she saw the patio doors sliding open as somebody stepped outside.

It was Aaron, her father-in-law. She hesitated, but then Carmen's words echoed in her head.

'An opportunity will come along. Give him a good view of your pussy and your tits and ass. Give him a lap dance if you must. He won't be able to resist the siren call'.

This was the opportunity.

She finished climbing onto the terrace and stood at the rim of the pool, dripping water.

When Aaron saw her, he stopped but then he kept on walking.

"I see you're naked," he said, openly staring at her nude form.

"It's hot and I was alone." She slurred her words, pretending to be tipsy. Giggling, she said, "I'm afraid I drank too much wine. Would you like a drink?"

"Sure. Bring me a bottle of brandy."

"Right away. Make yourself comfortable on one of the lounges. I'll be back shortly." She headed for the patio doors with swinging hips, knowing he was watching her naked buttocks. Inside the sunroom, she began to have sudden doubts about what she was planning, but then she shrugged. She was ready to do anything to secure her future. She grabbed a brandy bottle and a glass. Making a quick decision, she also took a bottle of wine for herself from the wine rack. Then she went back outside.

Aaron had taken off his shirt and lay on one of the lounges with a bare upper body. He sat up when she approached. "I figured I might as well soak up a little sun while I'm here. By the way, where is Allan?"

139

"He left for a business meeting. Won't be back before midnight." She poured the brandy into the glass and handed it to him. He sipped from it and looked at her over the rim of the glass. "You have a trim body," her murmured.

"Thank you. I work out." She sat down on the lounge across from him. "Keeps my body in shape and strong, especially my thighs." She reached over to grab his hand. "Here, touch them. They are strong and yet still soft."

Hesitating, he let her pull his hand toward her thigh. She shuddered a little when he touched her. Letting her thighs fall open, she gave him a healthy view of her pussy. Giggling again, she said with a seductive voice, "Everything on my body is soft but firm." She reached for the bottle of wine and took a mouthful, letting it dribble down her throat. Some of it ran down her chest.

"Are you drunk," Aaron asked without removing his hand from her thigh.

"Maybe just a little. I think I'll put this bottle out of reach before I drink so much I won't know what I'm doing." She slid from the lounge and bent to put down the bottle, pushing up her rump to let him see her thick pussy-lips. She heard him suck in his breath and exhale again with an audible sound. Getting onto her knees, she pretended to steady the bottle to keep it from falling, pushing her buttocks even higher. "I'm afraid I'm more than just a little drunk," she said, laughing.

"Are you sure Allan won't be back soon?" Aaron asked behind her with a strained voice.

She turned around and looked at him with large eyes. "I'm sure. He left me all alone. Poor little old

140

me is starved for the company of a strong, virile man."

She rose to her feet and stood swaying a little. Pretending to lose her balance, she fell forward and landed in his lap. "Oops." She smiled when she felt his hardness pressing into her. Wiggling her buttocks, she opened her legs to let his erect penis slide into the opening. "What is this?"

"You know what it is, you little bitch."

"Is that for me?"

"Get off my lap and bent across that lounge," he commanded harshly.

She obeyed his wish. Looking back over her shoulder, she watched him remove his pants. When he cupped her from the back, she was more than ready for him. She gave a little cry when he slid easily into her. Reaching around, he grabbed her breasts and held onto them as he rocked behind her. Arching her back, she pumped her buttocks and milked his hard penis vigorously. She had to admit, he had more stamina than she expected. He brought her to a number of orgasms before he shuddered between her quivering buttocks. She heard him shout hoarsely as he climaxed inside her, his fingers digging almost painfully into her breasts. She became aware of mewling sounds, realized they came from her own throat.

Collapsing on top of her, still holding onto her breasts, his breath came out in loud gasps.

"Wow!" he finally rasped. "I did not expect this. I can't remember the last time I had a climax this long and this high. Allan is a lucky son-of-a-bitch."

"You tell him," she said, trying to get her own breathing under control. "We haven't had sex for two years."

"I don't understand. I thought you had a happy marriage." He slipped from her and sat down on the lounge, still breathing heavily.

"It's an act." She sighed. "Ever since Andy died, Allan hasn't been the same. I don't think he loves me anymore. I don't know why. I never gave him a reason. It isn't my fault Andy died, even though he and Liz blamed me. They even accused me of having an affair with Andy. Nothing could have been further from the truth. He was my riding partner, which was all."

"I believe you. I never for a moment blamed you, and neither did Elke. I miss him, too, but life goes on. I think about him every day, but I don't let it interfere with my work and my relationships." He smiled. "Why didn't you confide in me earlier? I wouldn't have minded consoling you."

She gave him a crooked smile. "You're my father-in-law, for goodness sakes. I can't come to you with my sexual problems. What we did today was morally wrong."

He laughed. "According to whom? We're both consenting adults. I didn't rape you." He chuckled. "In fact it was you who seduced me." Before she could comment, he lifted a hand. "We're both guilty here, Claire. I have to admit, I've had the hots for you ever since Allan brought you home for the first time."

"I know. A woman notices things like that."

142

He reached for the brandy bottle. "I believe I need another drink." He took a swig from the bottle. "Lie down on the lounge, on your back."

With a questioning look, she asked, "What have you got in mind?"

"You'll see. I promise it won't hurt."

She stretched out on the lounge. He took the bottle and poured brandy onto her breasts and down her belly. Then he bent over her and began licking her breasts. Sliding his tongue across her belly, he moved between her legs and put his tongue into her slit. She moaned softly as she felt the pleasure building inside her and cried out when her body was racked by an unexpected orgasm.

Surprised, she watched Aaron slide on top of her and between her spread legs. His penis was hard and solid when he entered her. He took his time before he erupted inside her again. This time, he kissed her with great passion, and she returned his kisses.

Afterward, they lay like two lovers in each other's arms, glowing from the pleasures they both had given each other. When they separated, he rose and stood beside the lounge, looking down at her. "Nobody must ever know about this," he said.

"I agree. It is nobody's business. This will be our secret." She smiled.

"Get dressed. I'll take you out for supper. It won't raise anyone's suspicion when a man takes his beautiful daughter-in-law to a restaurant. At least it shouldn't."

* * *

143

Carmen called the next day, wondering if Claire was in the mood to go riding to the ranch. "I'll pick you up, girlfriend. Be ready."

Claire was bursting inside to tell Carmen about what happened between her and her father-in-law. Even though she had promised Aaron not to tell anyone, she reasoned it was Carmen's right to know. After all, the whole thing had been her idea in the first place.

"I had sex with Allan father yester afternoon," she said, trying to sound nonchalant.

Carmen gave her a surprised look from under dark lashes. "You had sex with your father-in-law?"

Claire nodded with a smug smile. "That's what I said."

"I'll be…" Carmen seemed to have a problem believing it. "You're not pulling my leg, are you?"

Claire laughed and moved her hand in front of her chest. "Cross my heart and hope to die."

"I haven't heard that expression in ages. It must be true, then."

"Believe me, it is."

"Judging from the glowing mood you're in, I assume it was satisfying."

"It was." Claire giggled like a teenage girl. "He was like a young stud and surpassed my expectations."

"How did you manage do get him to do it?"

Claire shrugged. "It was almost too easy."

"I'm proud of you, girl. Remember, what I said. Don't let it cool down. Keep on fucking him until you have him under your spell."

"Don't make it sound so crude, Carmen. At first, I almost felt guilty for seducing him the way I

144

did, but he was gentle and almost loving. He confessed his attraction for me and I knew I had nothing to feel sorry for. I gave him what he craved and he made me feel good. There are no villains here, only two people who spent an afternoon filled with passion in each other's arms." She smiled. "And a great deal of lust that needed to be fed."

Carmen laughed. "I think most of it was the latter. Just remember, he's twenty-five years older than you. He could be your father."

"He could be but he isn't. He's a fifty-five year old virile man and a better lover with more stamina than guys half his age. I speak from experience. I've made love to younger men that couldn't even keep it up for fifteen minutes. Before I got started, they were finished. Not so Aaron. We did it twice, and I have a suspicion, he would have been able to go another round."

She closed her eyes trying to recall the feeling he created in her when he licked the brandy off her body. Nobody had ever done that to her.

145

Chapter Nine

Aaron shuddered between her clutching thighs and left her embrace to lie on his back beside her, his breath coming in great gasps. "You'll kill me one of these days with your passion," he gasped. "You're insatiable. Where do you get all this energy?"

She laughed and rolled on top of him, kissing him gently. "You forget I'm much younger than you, old man."

He slapped her on the rump. "Don't call me 'old man'. I've still got plenty of years and juice left in me, little girl. I challenge any younger man to keep up with me."

She pouted. "I won't call you 'old man' if you stop calling me 'little girl'. I'm thirty years old."

He kissed her on the nose and chuckled. "Almost mature."

She slipped from the bed and padded across the tiled floor to the bathroom. Before she entered the bathroom, she turned and said, "I was thinking. Maybe we should go to another hotel from now on. It seems to me, the guy behind the front desk is beginning to wonder about us. This is the fifth time we've booked a room here. He might do some research and discover who you are. Aren't you worried about that?"

"Not really. So what if he does? What's he going to do with that information?"

She lifted her shoulders. "I don't know. Blackmail you?"

"Let him try. I have friends in the police department."

"That's good. I just thought I might mention it."

"Don't worry your pretty little head over that and let me handle it. Go, get yourself cleaned up. I want you to come to the races with me this afternoon. You'll be my good-luck-charm."

When she stood in front of the mirror, she took a good look at herself.

His 'good-luck-charm'. What happened? It seemed she's become nothing but his little whore. A trophy he liked to display without making their real relationship obvious. She might be walking down a dangerous road, a road she had chosen to walk all by herself, and there was no turning back. What kind of future waited for her? What would happen if she broke up with him? She didn't think he'd accept it lightly.

Stepping into the shower, she closed her eyes and let the warm water cleanse and soothe her body. The problem was she enjoyed the sex with Aaron. Sure, she was much younger, but this was not the first time she'd had sex with elderly men. Some of them had been so old she wondered, now that she was older, how they had survived having sex with her as a young teenager. She smiled. She had been wild and given them a good workout. Many had walked away on wobbly legs. It never occurred to her they might collapse and die on the spot.

Nothing had changed since those days. She had played a dangerous game then and was still playing it, except now her life may be on the line.

Aaron was still lounging in bed when she returned into the room, still naked.

"Don't move," he said. "Just stand there and let me admire your beautiful young body for a while. My wife used to have a trim body like yours." He sighed. "But now she's thirty pounds overweight with lumps where there shouldn't be any." He chuckled. "I close my eyes when we have sex and picture one of those starlets that come to my parties."

He threw back the covers. "I feel like dragging you back to bed, but I think I'd better take my shower now. We don't have much time to get down to the racetrack. Make no plans for tomorrow. We'll come back here and spend the whole day. I feel horny and energetic." He laughed. "Must be the weather."

* * *

Aaron was in a somber mood when they met the next day in the hotel bar.

"What is it?" she inquired.

"Not here. Come into my car. We have a problem."

She followed him outside and to his car. They walked without talking. After they sat in the car, he pulled a large envelope out of his briefcase and shook out its contents.

She stared at the pictures. There were at least a dozen. They weren't crystal clear, but clear enough to recognize her and Aaron in various positions on a bed.

"How?"

"All of them were taken from somewhere up in the ceiling above the bed in the hotel room."

"We would have seen a camera. At least I would have, lying on my back. How can you hide a camera on a ceiling?"

"They make them as small as buttons these days. A camera can easily be hidden in a smoke detector or light fixture."

"Who sent these to you?"

"I don't know. Aside from the pictures there was a note attached. Here, look at this."

It was just a piece of paper with the words 'I want 2 million dollars or these pictures go public. I will contact you. Do not go to the police'. The words were written with letters cut out from newspaper headlines.

She stared at him. "We can't have Allan or your wife see these pictures. Or any of your business associates. What are we going to do? Will you give in to their demands?"

"Not if I can help it. Do you have any idea who could be behind this? I mean, who would be watching us?"

"You must have dozens of enemies who'd like nothing better than to discredit you. Remember, someone broke into your computer."

"I remember, but nothing came out of that yet. Are you sure there is nobody who has a grudge against you?"

"Well, there might be someone. A few weeks ago, my girlfriend and I saw two men drown another man. They tried to intimidate me."

"Who are these men?"

She hesitated. "You won't like the answer. One of them is a cop by the name of Ron Salsky. You know the other man. You're in business with his boss, Mister Tanaka."

"Are you talking about his lawyer, Mohan Bakshi? Somehow I can't believe that. Did you go to the police with your suspicion?"

"No, I didn't. I told Allan about it and he warned me against making big waves and in the process killing his deal with Tanaka. I also got threatened by Salsky and Bakshi. They promised to cut up my face with a razorblade. I took those threats seriously."

"You are sure about what you saw?"

"I am. If I still had doubts, they disappeared when they threatened me. They also said it would be useless to go to the police, because Salsky is a well-respected cop with friends in high places. Cops stick together."

"That may be true. The police commissioner and I have a good relationship. I can make inquiries. Do you remember when this alleged murder took place?"

"I remember it clearly." She told him and he jotted it down in a little notebook he carried. "I even have a partial name of the man they drowned. His first name was Joe."

"That may help." He wrote that down also. "I don't trust my memory and neither do I trust my cell phone." He gave her a sad smile. "I think we should postpone our date. Right now, I'm not quite in the mood."

She returned his smile. "Neither am I." Touching his hand, she became serious. "I'm

150

scared. I don't believe these men play games. They are ruthless. I hope these inquiries will be done discreetly without arousing suspicion."

"It all depends on what they find. Don't worry. We're in the same boat here. I will hire a detective to investigate this Bakshi and, of course, Tanaka and his company. I should have done that before I began doing business with him. I'm going to see the Commissioner today. Be careful driving home and be aware of your surroundings."

"I'll be careful." She blew him a kiss and left his car. When she walked to her own car, she kept looking around, feeling watched and on edge. She cursed the day when she saw Bakshi and Salsky by the lake. She and Carmen should have minded their own business and left things well enough alone.

She called Carmen from her car phone. Carmen didn't answer so she left a message. "I need to see you, Carmen. It is urgent. Call me back."

Her phone rang only a few minutes later. "What's the emergency?"

"I can't discuss it over the phone. Can you meet me right away?"

"Where?"

"At the ranch."

"The ranch? You want to go riding?"

"Yes, I do. I need to clear my head."

"Okay, if that's what you want. I don't really see the urgency."

"Just meet me." She cut the connection. Feeling irritated and jittery, she realized she was driving way past the speed limit. 'Maybe I should just end it. Then everything would be resolved'. Slowing down, she suddenly suffered from a

151

laughing spell. 'With my luck I'd probably demolish my car and half a dozen others, break my back and end up in a wheelchair'.

"Take it easy, girl," she said to herself. "You're hysteric. Aaron will fix this."

Randy was surprised to see her. "This is so unexpected. What's the occasion?"

"Nothing special. It's a beautiful day and I was lonely, so I thought it would be a great opportunity to give Black Lightening a workout. By the way, Carmen should be here soon."

"Oh." He looked disappointed. "I thought you may have come to see me. You haven't been around."

"I'm sorry. I've been busy. I flew to Rocktown for a few days to visit my parents and to go to the funeral of a friend."

"Sorry to hear that. Your parents are okay? Healthy?"

She nodded. "Yes to both questions. They scolded me for not visiting them all these years, and I can't blame them for being unhappy." She turned when she heard a car driving onto the lot. "There's Carmen."

Carmen gave her a hug. To Randy she said, "Hi Randy. Have you been taking good care of my horse?"

He grinned. "No. I've been neglecting it. Hay is getting expensive and I had to cut down on the feedings."

"Sure. I don't see any shortage of grass." She smiled. "I'd take my horse elsewhere in a heartbeat if your dad and mine hadn't been such good friends.

I guess, Claire told you she wants to go riding. We do need the horses for that."

He touched his cap. "Right away, my Lady. I'll have Larry get them for you. Why not go into the house until he's ready? I'll meet you for a drink."

Claire was still feeling a little jittery, but having Carmen with her helped to calm her down.

"What's this all about?" Carmen asked as they walked toward the house.

"Aaron is being blackmailed. Somebody took pictures of him and me in compromising positions, if you know what I mean."

"Somebody photographed you and Aaron while you were having sex? Whose idea was that?"

Claire gave Carmen a surprised look. "Are you thinking Aaron hired a photographer?"

"No?"

"Of course not. The pictures were taken with a hidden camera in the hotel room. Whoever took them, wants two million dollars or they go public."

"You suspect anyone?"

"Yes. Either Salsky or Bakshi. Most likely both of them. They must have put a tail on either me or Aaron and found out about our relationship." She rubbed her forehead, hoping she wouldn't get a headache. "I wish I'd never started with Aaron. I should have known it would not end well."

Carmen reached out and took Claire into her arms. "It's not your fault. I was the one who suggested it. Blame me if you need to blame someone."

"I'm not blaming you, Carmen. I'm a grown woman and make my own decisions. Nobody forced me to do it."

"What's wrong?" It was Randy who came through the door.

Claire disengaged herself from Carmen. "I think I'm getting a headache. Carmen was just consoling me."

"I could console you. I have a good recipe for a headache." Randy chuckled merrily.

Claire smiled. "I know your recipes. I would take you up on it any other time, but not today. Are the horses ready?"

"Give Larry a few more minutes. Have that drink with me and relax. There is still enough daylight left for you to go for a ride."

Claire felt better after a couple of drinks. "You should come by more often," Randy said. "I miss you."

"Maybe I will." She rose. "Thanks for the drink. Let's go, Carmen, I'm getting restless."

It felt good to sit in the saddle and let the horse run across the field of grass. Black Lightning seemed to enjoy it also and she didn't hold him back. Carmen tried to keep up with them, but her horse fell behind.

After a while, Claire slowed down the stallion to let Carmen catch up. She felt elated, as if she had been the one running.

"I get the impression you both needed this," Carmen commented as she pulled up beside Claire. "Feeling better?"

"Yes. Much."

Randy asked her to stay, but she declined. "Perhaps another time. Right now, I got a lot of stuff happening. It wouldn't be good."

"Alright. I'm a patient man."

154

Someone must have been watching her house. When she drove into the driveway and before she entered the garage, a kid came running and banged on her window. When she opened it, he handed her an envelope. As he turned to run away, she asked, "Who gave you this envelope?"

The kid lifted his thin shoulders. "I don't know. Some guy. He gave me ten bucks and told me to give it to you."

"What did he look like?"

"I didn't get a good look at him. He was in a black car. That's all I know."

He ran away before she could ask more questions. She didn't have to guess what the envelope contained. Her suspicion was confirmed when she pulled out the pictures with shaking hands. The demand on the note only asked for one million dollars. They might have asked for ten million. She couldn't get her hands on one million dollars and she certainly couldn't talk to Allan about it.

* * *

Aaron called her in the afternoon the next day.

"I spoke to the Commissioner yesterday. He did me a favor and looked into what you told me. There actually was an incident around that time. A couple of days after the date you mentioned, a drug dealer by the name of Joe Moretti washed up near the Midtown Bridge. The file said he may have committed suicide or he fell accidentally into the river and drowned. There was no reason to suspect foul play. He said he wants to talk to you and get

155

your statement. I'll have someone pick you up tomorrow at nine o'clock to take you to the Commissioner's office."

"You won't be there?"

"No. I have to go to a meeting, but I'll talk to you later."

"Has anyone contacted you yet?"

"Nothing so far. It seems they're biding their time. I have no doubt they'll contact me soon."

"They sent me the same pictures with a demand for one million dollars," she told him.

"This means they know who you are and where you live. Your life may be in danger. The Commissioner promised to investigate this Salsky. In the meantime, I will try to find out more about Bakshi."

She had trouble sleeping that night, but she slept in the next day. When she went down to have breakfast, Allan was long gone. It didn't matter, because she couldn't confide in him anyway.

At nine o'clock, a car driven by Aaron's chauffeur picked her up and took her to the Commissioner's office. She told the chauffeur to wait for her before she entered the building. Her interview with the Commissioner didn't take long. After telling him what she and Carmen saw that day, he said, "You are certain it was Ron Salsky?"

"Quite certain."

"How about the other man?"

She nodded. "Yes, I am."

"Do you know either of these two men personally?"

"I didn't then, but now I know Mister Bakshi."

"How do you know him?"

156

"He works for a Mister Tanaka. My husband and my father-in-law are doing business with him. Bakshi is Mister Tanaka's lawyer."

"I see. Mister Belmont said these two men threatened you. What did they say?"

"They threatened to disfigure my face with a razor blade if I were to go to the police. That was only one thing they said. There was more. Nothing pleasant."

"Would you testify in court if you had to?"

"Yes, I would, but only if I'm guaranteed protection and these men get punished."

"If they are guilty and it can be proven, they will go away for a long time. Thank you, Missis Belmont. We'll keep you informed."

After the chauffeur dropped her off again at home, she drove to have lunch at a small diner. She didn't want to go home after lunch, feeling jittery, alone, and scared, so she decided to drive to the gym where she would be among other people.

After spending an hour using different machines and a nice hot shower she felt better. That good feeling changed when a car pulled up beside her as she walked to her car in the parking lot.

It was Bakshi. He got out of his car. "You've been a bad girl, Claire. You went to the police, even though we warned you. My buddy Ron is not happy. He's being investigated. His reputation is at stake here and we can't have that."

"You should have thought about that before you sent me a ransom note," she said haughtily.

"I have absolutely no idea what you're talking about."

157

"I bet you don't. Now, leave me alone." She began walking toward her car.

He walked beside her and put an arm around her shoulder. "Let me give you a friendly warning. If you stick to your story, there will be consequences. Should you decide to testify in a court of law, I promise you that you will be killed. You and your girlfriend. Do you understand?"

A cold shiver ran down Claire's back as he voiced his threat. "You can't threaten me, you bastard," she hissed.

"Oh yes, I can and I am. I could kill you right here, should I decide it necessary, but I won't. Actually, I was hoping you and I could get together for an evening of fun and excitement. I enjoyed our little episode in your father-in-law's office and I know you did, too. I wouldn't mind sampling that tight, hot pussy of yours for a whole night. Wouldn't you like that?"

"You're a sick son-of-a-bitch. You won't get away with this, I promise." She rammed her elbow into his chest and ran away. Her car was not far. She pushed her remote while she ran and ripped open the door of her car. Sliding onto the seat, she slammed her door shut and sat breathing hard.

Bakshi had not followed her as she feared. She didn't even see his car.

Her knees were shaking and her legs felt like rubber. She sat for a long time before she found the strength to drive away.

That evening, she called Randy and asked if she could come to his ranch for a few days.

Chapter Ten

Randy was obviously surprised to see her again so soon. He greeted her with, "Everything okay at home?"

She shook her head. "No. I'm in trouble and I don't know what to do. You're the only friend I have who I can trust and who isn't involved."

"That sounds ominous. Come into the house and tell me all about it."

He took her into his office. "It's the only place where we can talk undisturbed. I assume what you have to tell me is private?"

"It is." She sat in one of the two chairs. He took the other one and leaned forward.

"Okay. What's this all about?"

"I don't know how to tell you this, but I made a stupid mistake." She paused, trying to decide how much she should tell him.

"Okay. We all make mistakes. What's so stupid about this one?"

"I had sex with someone I shouldn't have. Somebody took photos of us and now we're being blackmailed. They want one million dollars from me."

He sat silent for a moment.

"Are you disappointed in me?"

"Disappointed?"

"Because I had sex with some other guy?"

He shrugged. "You and I are not married. I'm not your keeper."

"I can see it in your eyes that you are not happy."

He chuckled. "No, I'm not happy, but like I said we're not a couple. Who did you have sex with?"

"It doesn't matter. Let's just say it was stupid of me. I had a reason for doing it, but that is neither here nor there now."

"Have you gone to the police?"

"I have, but with another matter, which is most likely connected to this whole fiasco."

"I don't understand."

"Remember, a few weeks ago when Carmen and I told you about the murder we witnessed?"

"You assumed you witnessed. We're talking about Salsky, right? Are you saying he's the one blackmailing you?"

"I'm not certain if he is the blackmailer, but I suspect his buddy, Mohan Bakshi. Salsky is probably involved, also. Bakshi threatened to kill me if I testified in court against him and Salsky. I know for a fact that a drug dealer by the name of Joe Moretti washed up on the shore of the river a few days after Carmen and I saw Salsky and Bakshi drown a guy they called Joe. According to their story, he hit his head, fell into the water and drowned. They never filed a report."

"That certainly puts a different twist to your story. Why would they threaten you if they're innocent? However, just because they threatened you, doesn't mean they are the blackmailers."

"Who else would be interested in my activities?"

"Allan?"

160

"I don't believe that. He doesn't care what I do. All I know is that somebody followed me to the hotel where I...where I had sex with this other man."

"Obviously, you went there more than once. You gave them the perfect opportunity to install a camera." He smiled crookedly. "Had I been that man, I wouldn't have made such a mistake. You don't go to the same place twice in a row. You're only inviting trouble."

"Sounds like you have experience in that department."

"Not really, at least not in the sex-department. I'm an ex-marine and I had some training on how to stay invisible. Besides, it only makes sense. How about the man you were with? Did he receive a ransom note?"

"He did. They want two million dollars from him."

"Is it possible you weren't even the target? Maybe he's the one."

"It could be possible, but that's highly unlikely."

"We can't rule out anything." He regarded her solemnly. "What are you planning to do? Will you pay the ransom?"

"I can't get my hands on one million dollars."

"If you want to find out if this Bakshi is the blackmailer, we have to set a trap," he mused.

"How?"

"Have you been contacted aside from the original note?"

"No."

161

"When he contacts you with instructions, you insist you will meet him in a place of your choosing, like a hotel room. I'll be there with you, and when he shows up we'll confront him."

Somehow she wasn't enthusiastic about that idea. "What will you do with him? Kill him?"

His smile didn't convey any humor. "Nothing so drastic, unless things go sideways."

"I'd rather not get involved in a murder." She shook herself.

"It wouldn't be murder. I'd kill him only in self-defence. Let's hope it won't come to that. Do you have a better idea?"

"I don't. Why don't we give it a few days and mull it over, okay?"

"There is nothing we can do now anyway, not until he contacts you. By the way, have you eaten?"

"Not since breakfast."

"Good. I'll have Carlos prepare a nice lunch for us. You can order anything you want. He'll be happy to oblige." He patted his belly. "Carlos is a genius in the kitchen. I haven't eaten this well for a long time. Nothing but gourmet food. I'm afraid I'm gaining weight."

She chuckled. "Perhaps you need to work out. Tomorrow, we'll start a rigorous exercise program to get you on the right track."

He grinned. "As long as it involves two people exercising together, I won't object."

She slapped him on the arm. "I can just imagine what kind of exercise you have in mind."

"How can I not imagine it? I've missed you."

She was contacted two days later. When she answered her cell, a voice that was obviously distorted, told her it was time to pay the ransom and gave her a location where she should drop of the money. She wasn't a hundred percent sure if it was Bakshi, but she thought she detected some sort of accent.

"Let's not play games," she said. "I don't trust you and won't meet you there. By the way, I know it is you, Bakshi, so don't hide behind this ridiculous sounding voice. You said you wanted to have a night of fun with me? Well, here is your chance. I can only raise three-quarter-million dollars, but I'm willing to spend a night with you in a hotel room of my choice. I'll do anything you want. I promise to give you the best time of your life. You won't regret it."

There was a pause before the voice continued. "I think you have me confused with someone else. I'm not this Bakshi guy, but I'll accept your offer. It will be an expensive night, and it better be worth it. When and where do you want to meet?"

"Make it two days from now. Eight o'clock at the Marquise. I'll wait for you by the bar. How will I recognize you if you're not Bakshi?"

"Don't worry about that. I know what you look like. I'll find you. One word of warning. No funny business. If I smell a rat, all bets are off, and you will regret it."

"No funny business. I promise."

She put down the phone and took a few deep breaths. "I guess the moment of truth is coming. He denies being Bakshi, but I don't believe him. I still say it is him."

"You'll find out in a couple of days." Randy looked thoughtful. "You realize much can go wrong

163

with this plan. I hope you're prepared for what might happen. If you're not then we shouldn't go through with it."

"What else can I do except pay the ransom? I don't have the money."

"How about the guy you…?" He didn't finish.

"The guy I screwed?" She lifted one shoulder. "He's got the money, but that isn't the point. I don't like being blackmailed. Bakshi must be held responsible for what he's putting me through. I don't care what you do to him. Beat him up, kill him if you must," she said fiercely. Then she put her face between her hands and sobbed. "What's happening to me? I'm not this violent person. It was never supposed to get this far. All I want is to get away from Allan without sacrificing my future."

"If you're so unhappy you should leave him. You're young enough to get married again."

With a sigh, she said, "I can't. He'll never give me a divorce."

"Then move in with someone." He grinned. "I'm game."

She gave him a sad smile. "You're sweet and I love you, but that is not the solution to my problem."

"I'd give you all my love and protect you from harm. You would never want for anything, and your future would be secure. Isn't that what you want?"

"Of course it is, but I would always feel I'm cheating on my husband, which would actually be true. I'd like to start my new life with a clean slate, without obligations and a guilty conscience."

"Don't we all?" His eyes expressed sadness. "Life isn't perfect. We've all done things we regret, things we wish had turned out differently. There is nothing we can do about that but except them and move on. We must make the best of what destiny has put on our plate. Life is too short to live in constant misery. Sometimes we must make a drastic break to change a future that seems so certain. Nothing is impossible." He reached out to touch her cheek. "Let's go and visit Carlos in the kitchen. We'll have a scrumptious lunch and then we'll get on our horses and spend the afternoon enjoying the fresh air and taking in the sights."

She gave him a little smile. "That sounds good to me."

* * *

Two days later, they rented a suite at the Marquise. Randy hid in the bedroom while Claire went down to the bar to wait for her contact. She was certain it would be Bakshi.

She wasn't disappointed. He walked in at exactly eight o'clock. When he spotted her sitting at the bar, he scanned the room and then headed for her.

She forced herself to give him a friendly smile. "I was right. It was you."

He took the stool beside her. "Did you bring the money?"

"I did. It is in the suite I rented."

"I've changed my mind. Go and get the money. We'll make the transfer in my car."

"How about my other offer?"

"I'll accept that also, but not here. I don't trust you. We'll drive to another hotel."

165

She panicked a little and thought frantically how she could get him to come to the room with her. "Forgive me if I don't trust you, either. I'm not going to another hotel with you. I won't take the chance of ending up dead in some back alley."

"If I wanted to kill you, you'd be dead already. It's either that or the deal is off. Those pictures will be published."

"You'll never see any money. I promise you that. What are you afraid of, anyway? I can't overpower you physically. There are no cameras in that room. All that is waiting for you is a night of passion. You want to know something? I did enjoy that evening in my father-in-law's office. You're an attractive, capable man, and I was looking forward to this. Don't look a gift horse in the mouth. You have nothing to lose if you accept my offer. Besides, you'll also get three-quarter-million dollars. There are no strings attached, except that I want those pictures. However, it won't happen unless it happens here. I won't change my mind."

He seemed to mull over what she told him, giving her hope he might give in. "I have a gun," he finally said."

"You won't need a gun. I'm unarmed. I don't even know how to use a gun. Guns scare me."

"Good. Then let's go."

He followed her to the suite. She swiped the entry keypad with her card and pushed open the door.

"You first," he said, brandishing a gun.

"I told you, a gun is not necessary."

"I never take chances. Now go in."

166

She stepped across the threshold and walked straight to the small chesterfield, sinking into it. He took a couple of cautious steps into the room and looked around, the gun in his hand.

"You're sure a paranoid person," she said with a forced laugh, trying frantically to come up with an idea to make him put down the gun.

"I've learned a long time ago not to trust anyone, especially not a woman."

"Well, you can trust me." She removed her jacket and unbuttoned her blouse. "You want to take off my bra? You guys like that."

"Is this some kind of trick?"

She rose and walked toward him with a sexy smile. "Yes, it is. I want you to get into the mood."

Standing in front of him, she looked into his face. "Why are you so reluctant? Don't wait until I cool down again. Right now, I'm really horny."

"You're a teasing bitch." He grabbed and kissed her roughly.

She broke the kiss and stepped back. Reaching behind her, she undid the bra-strep and let her breasts tumble out. "Let's go into the bedroom," she whispered huskily. "I prefer a bed when I have sex."

"You first," he said, gesturing with the gun.

Walking through the door into the other room, she didn't see Randy and hoped he hadn't left for some reason. Turning around, she said, "Come in. No cameras in here, either."

He followed, reluctantly, it seemed. She went to sit on the bed. He stood in front of her. "Get naked," he commanded.

When she stood nude in front of him, she pouted. "How about you? Are you going to put that

167

gun away or are you planning to wave it around while we have sex? What if it goes off accidentally? I don't feel like dying that was."

"All in good time." He studied her body. "I can't see any wires, so I guess you're clean." He put the gun on the night table and began to undress.

'Now would be a good time for you to appear, Randy'.

"Turn around and bend over," Bakshi said.

"I like it lying on my back," she protested.

"And I like taking a woman from behind. Now, do it!"

She turned and bent forward, her upper body resting on the bed, her buttocks facing him. He moved behind her and put his hand between her legs, spreading them wider.

This was not the way she had planned. She had been prepared to get undressed, especially when he produced the gun, but her plan never included to actually have sex with him. Where the hell was Randy?

When she felt what, obviously, was his rigid penis touching the entrance to her vagina, she panicked. Twisting around, she stared up at him. "I've never liked it that way. It's so impersonal. Let's move onto the bed and do it properly. I want to feel your body on top of me with your arms around me, and I want to look into your eyes when you come inside me."

"We can do that later, but right now we'll do it my way. Turn around, spread your legs and let me enter!"

She just about followed his demand, when she saw Randy appear behind Bakshi. Bakshi stiffened, and then he fell forward to end up on the bed, barely missing Claire. She rolled out of the way and off the bed, to stand trembling at the foot of the bed. That had been much too close.

Randy was on top of Bakshi, twisting his arm behind his back and pressing him facedown into the mattress. Letting go of Bakshi's arm, Randy stepped back, a gun in his hand.

Bakshi turned and sat up. "Who the hell are you?"

"I'm the guy who will put a bullet between your eyes if you insist on bothering and threatening Claire."

"What's it to you?" Bakshi watched Randy with a calculating look in his eyes. Without a warning, he lunged forward and pushed Randy off balance.

Both men fell to the floor with Bakshi smashing his fist into Randy's face. Things went fast after that.

Claire feared Bakshi might gain the upper hand, but her fears were unfounded. It was clear from the onset that Bakshi had no chance. Once Randy was done with him, Bakshi's face was covered with blood, and it was obvious his upper body would be featuring many colorful spots in the next few days. Claire almost felt sorry for him, but only almost. He deserved what he got.

Randy stood over Bakshi and glared at him. "Thank your lucky stars I didn't break any of your bones. You threaten Claire again or should you use those pictures you claim you have in any way, it won't end well for you." He kicked Bakshi in the

169

side. "By the way, I'm taking your gun to the police. Who knows what they'll find."

"Go to hell," Bakshi cursed, spitting blood. "This isn't over."

"It better be, for your own good, unless you have a death wish." He glanced at Claire. "Get dressed."

Claire went into the other room and dressed in a hurry. She wanted to get out as fast as possible.

Randy came out of the bedroom, a serious look on his face. "I don't trust that bastard," he said. "Maybe you should come and stay at the ranch for a while."

170

Chapter Eleven

It happened three nights later. Claire had barely drifted off to sleep, when Randy shook her awake. "I heard a car pull up," he said in a low voice. "I'm not expecting any visitors."

"Maybe it's one of your employees."

He shook his head. "It's the weekend. They all went home. Missis Collins doesn't drive, and her sons don't go anywhere. I'm going to investigate."

Claire slipped out of bed. "I'm coming with you."

"I think it's best if you stay in the house." He put on his shirt and pants.

A couple of short popping sounds caused him to curse. "Those were gunshots, damn it. Whoever is out there didn't come for a friendly visit." He went to his gun-cabinet and took out a rifle and a box of ammo. After loading the rifle, he rushed out the door.

She went down to the main floor and walked to the living room window. It was dark outside, but the yard light illuminated a car near the stable. Then she heard another popping sound and almost immediately after that two more gunshots in rapid succession. They sounded different from those other ones.

Even though Randy told Claire to stay behind, she needed to know what happened. Taking a coat out of the closet, she slipped into it and hurried outside. Everything was quiet now. A figure appeared in the open door of the stable and walked out slowly. Whoever it was, carried a rifle, and then she recognized Randy. Breathing a sigh of relief, she ran toward him. "What happened?"

He didn't answer right away. When he answered his words came out strained. "Those bastards killed two of my horses. Then they shot me."

"Oh my god," she gasped. "Are you hurt badly?"

"I don't know. They got me in my left arm. It hurts like hell."

"Let's get back into the house so I can have a look at it." She shivered, fearing the worst. "How many are there?"

"Two men."

"I heard two rifle-shots."

"That's all I needed. We have to call the police. It was self-defence."

"You shot both of them? Are they dead?"

"I'm afraid so."

They reached the house and went into the kitchen. Randy's left shirtsleeve was dark with blood.

"Sit down," she told him. He pulled up one of the kitchen chairs and sat on it, still clinging to his rifle. She took it from his hands and laid it on the table. "I don't think you need that in here," she said gently. "Let's take off your shirt."

She unbuttoned it for him and pulled it off. The blood seeped from a wound on his upper arm. "I think it's only a flesh wound. It looks worse than it is. You were lucky, the bullet only grazed you. I'll have to clean and bandage it. I hope you have a first aid kit."

"In the upstairs bathroom."

"I'll get it." She rushed upstairs, relieved Randy was okay. She found the first-aid-kit in the cupboard and a bottle of disinfecting solution. Hurrying back down, she saw Randy standing by the kitchen sink, cleaning his arm with a cloth.

"Are you crazy? You don't want to get an infection. Let me do it."

"I only wanted to wash off my arm. The bleeding has already slowed to a trickle."

"Go, sit in that chair again," she commanded.

He grinned. "You can get quite bossy. I like that. It almost turns me on."

"Oh, you. Always making fun of me. Now, be a good boy and let me take care of your arm." She proceeded to clean the wound and the surrounding area with the disinfection solution. Then she applied some antibiotic cream and bandaged his arm. "I suggest you go to a hospital or your doctor in a few days to have a professional look at the wound. You may even need a tetanus shot." She shrugged. "I don't have any medical training. I only learned first aid."

"You're doing a fine job. Thank you. I'm going to take a painkiller and then I should be good until I see my doctor." He sighed. "I'm tired, but I'm afraid we won't get any rest for a while. It will be a long night. I have to call the State Police and report this unfortunate incident."

"While you do that, I'm going to get dressed. I don't want them to see me in my nightgown."

The two troopers didn't say much when they looked at the dead men in the barn. One of them walked over to where the two horses lay. "These two did that?"

"Yes, they did."

"Is that the reason you killed them?"

"I killed them in self-defence after they shot me. At that time, I didn't know yet about my dead horses."

"Why would they shoot your horses?"

"How would I know?"

"Do you know these two men?"

"I've never seen them in my life before this."

The trooper made a few notes in a little book. He looked up and said, "We'll have to get a forensics team in here. Don't touch anything until then."

"I have no intention to do so. Before I answer any more of your questions, do I need a lawyer?"

With a shrug, the other trooper said, "It may be advisable. After all, two men have been murdered."

"Not murdered. Shot in self-defence. There is a difference."

"So you claim, Mister…?"

"Forrest. Randy Forrest."

The trooper made more notes. Then he looked around. It seemed to Claire the trooper noticed her for the first time. "Were you present when this went down, Missis Forrest?"

"I'm not Missis Forrest. My name is Claire Belmont. No, I didn't witness the shooting, but I heard three shots from the inside of the house, where I was at the time."

"Is there a Missis Forrest?"

"I'm not married," Randy injected.

"I see. Are you a visitor here, Missis Belmont?"

"I board my horse at Mister Forrest's ranch. I come here often to ride my horse. Mister Forrest gives me riding lessons sometimes."

"Riding lessons." The trooper nodded. "Do you make it a habit of staying overnight, Missis Belmont?"

"No usually, but sometimes it gets too late. I don't like driving in the dark."

"Are you married, Missis Belmont?"

"Yes. My husband is Allan Belmont."

"Does your husband know you are here?"

The question seemed innocent enough, but Claire resented being questioned like a suspect. "Do I need a lawyer, also?"

"Not unless you're involved in this shooting."

"I'm not. I'm only a witness from afar."

The trooper turned back to Randy. "One last question. Do you have any idea why anyone would want to shoot the horses on your ranch? Any enemies you may have?"

"None I can think of at the moment."

"It doesn't make sense. I could understand it if they came to steal a horse, but then they would have come in a truck." He looked toward the barn door when the lights of another vehicle lit up the entrance. "It seems the forensics team is here. They'll take over the investigation. We'll be in touch, Mister Forrest. Don't go anywhere and don't leave the State. Let's go and get the rifle you used. We'll need it as evidence."

175

They accompanied Randy to the house. Claire didn't see any point in hanging around in the barn to watch the forensics team, so she went with them.

After the troopers left, Randy sat down on one of the chairs and wiped his forehead. "Do you know a good lawyer?"

"I do. He's an old friend, but he lives in Rocktown."

"That's okay. If he's interested, I'll hire him. I have a feeling those troopers are going to make trouble."

Claire went to the window and looked out. "There is another police vehicle there, probably from the city, also a couple of vans."

"One would be the coroner. I wonder why they called the city cops."

Claire turned away from the window. "You told the State trooper you have no idea who would want to do this. Don't you have any suspicions at all?"

"I do. That friend of yours comes to mind. He said it wasn't over and I didn't think so, either."

"Please, don't call him my friend," Claire said vehemently. "He's my worst nightmare. I wish I'd kept my mouth shut that day and ignored what I saw. This would never have happened." She came and stood in front of him. "I'm so sorry I brought this to you."

He reached out with his good arm and took her hand into his. "Don't blame yourself, Claire. You thought you did a good deed by reporting a murder. You meant well. How can anyone fault you for that? I brought this on myself when I got involved. There is one thing I'm not sure of. I can't believe that Ron Salsky is involved in all of this. I sort of know him. He's been coming here for years. Not often, but he does. He and another cop, actually. They rent a couple of horses and take them out for a ride. Why would he want to cause trouble on my ranch?"

"Just because he's a cop doesn't mean he's a good person. It wouldn't be the first time a cop is crooked. Remember, he was the other guy we saw in the water. Also, he and Bakshi seem to be friends. They're in this together, of that I'm certain." Claire pulled her hand away and sat down on one of the other chairs. "I'm tired. Do you think we can go back to bed?"

"I don't know. I'll stay up for a while longer, but you go. If there is anything I'll wake you."

"You're sure?"

"Quite. I wouldn't be able to sleep now, anyway."

"I don't know if I can, but I'll try." She got up, bent to give him a kiss, and went up to the bedroom. Getting undressed, she slipped into her nightgown again and crawled under the covers. Trying to relax, she found it next to impossible. She kept seeing the two dead men lying on the barn floor, their heads in a pool of blood. A shiver ran through her body when the thought occurred to her that it easily could have been Randy lying there. They may even have come into the house and shot her. Possibly, raped her first. Her mind was spinning, thinking about that.

She got up and went into the bathroom to look for something to calm her nerves. She found a bottle of Valium and took a pill. Hopefully, it would help her sleep.

She awoke when she felt the bed shake a little and realized Randy had joined her on the bed.

"Everything okay?" She reached out to touch him, reassured by his presence.

"Everything's fine. Go back to sleep."

* * *

Claire drove home the next day. Worried about Carmen, hoping she wouldn't be affected by all this, she wanted to talk to her but not on the phone. When she walked into the house, Allan confronted her.

"I got a call from the State Police, asking if I knew your whereabouts. I told them I had no idea where you'd disappeared to this time. I had to hear it from them that you spent your nights at the Black Stallion Ranch. They also told me about the shooting. It gives me cause to wonder what you are doing at that ranch. Are you fucking this Forrest?"

"What do you care if I did?" She tried to stay calm. It wouldn't do to lose her temper, especially since what he accused her of was true.

"You're my wife, and I have to worry about my reputation. It wouldn't do to have a slut for a wife."

"Your reputation? Is that all you care about? How about my welfare, my safety? Do you care about that at all?"

"Oh, just shut up! You disgust me." He walked away, heading for his office.

178

She stared after him, furious and feeling so helpless, hating him more than ever. She ran into her bedroom and threw herself on the bed, wishing this nightmare she was living would end. How did it ever get this far?

When her phone rang, it was Carmen. "I've been worried about you, girlfriend. Where have you been?"

In spite of her mood, Claire had to laugh.

"Did I say something funny?"

"I wish, but hearing your voice is so good. At least when you ask me where I've been it is out of concern, unlike when Allan asks it. Can you come over or are you busy?"

"I could be at your place in twenty minutes. Is that okay?"

"I'll be waiting outside."

She went outside and sat again on one of the planters in front of the house. It was a good place to sit and brood. Looking at the flowers and the flowering shrubs circling the driveway, didn't lift her mood. When Carmen's convertible appeared between the massive stone pillars, her mood had not changed.

"What's the matter?" Carmen always knew when she was in this dark mood. "You look like somebody died."

"Maybe I did and this is only my ghost walking around." Claire gave Carmen a hug. "Good to see you. I've had a bad week. Let's go to the back and I'll tell you all about it."

Carmen stayed silent for quite some time after Claire told her everything that happened since they

179

last they saw each other. Then she reached out and touched Claire's hand. "It seems ever since that afternoon down by the lake, one bad thing after another has happened to you. I feel partially responsible for some of it. I should have never suggested you have sex with your father-in-law, but I meant well."

"Don't blame yourself. You only suggested. It was my choice, and I have to admit, I enjoyed it." She smiled. "Aaron is a virile man. He knows how to make a girl happy." Her expression became serious again. "I dragged Randy into this. That makes the whole situation worse. Who knows, he may even be charged with involuntary manslaughter. He killed two men. Bakshi is a lawyer. If he's behind it, which I suspect, he will find some little unknown law to accuse Randy of something."

"You're right, Randy shot those men, but they killed a couple of his horses and wounded him. He shouldn't be charged with anything. It was clearly self-defence. A man should be able to protect his property. We have laws. After all, we live in America and not some third world country where this Bakshi comes from, one of those countries where the police and the politicians are corrupt and where good men and women get thrown in jail without good cause."

"We have plenty of corrupt cops, too. Salsky is probably one of them."

"Not all cops are bad, Claire. You told me he's being investigated. If he's guilty of anything, justice will be done. Your father-in-law has connections. Have you asked him to pay the ransom for you?"

"No, I haven't."

"Then you'd better ask him. It's in his best interest to make this thing go away." She got up from her lounge. "Let's get you out of this down-mood. The sun is shining. It is warm. We have a swimming pool just waiting for us. I'm going for a swim. Come on. It'll do you good." Carmen removed her top and pulled down her jeans. She was naked underneath. She laughed when she saw Claire's expression. "I didn't bring a bathing suit. Don't look so surprised. You've seen me naked before. Besides, this is your house. We're protected from view by all those trees and bushes. Don't gawk at me like some butch. Get undressed and join me in the pool." With that, she turned around and dove into the water.

Despite her gloomy mood, Claire had to laugh. It was good to have a friend like Carmen. She always did things spontaneously, crazy things sometimes. She shrugged and got undressed. Then she jumped into the pool.

Two days later, Allan came storming out of his office to confront Claire. "Tanaka just informed me he's pulling out of the deal. You stupid woman couldn't keep your mouth shut and accuse a good man of murder. Your stupidity is going to cost me millions."

"I warned you against going into business with him. Had you listened to me, you wouldn't be in this position now. Now who's the stupid one?"

He glared at her. "Don't call my stupid. It's entirely your fault. If you'd stay home the way a good wife does and not go riding that damn horse of

181

yours in the woods, you wouldn't have seen what you thought you saw."

"If you did your husbandly duty, the way a good husband does, I wouldn't have to go riding all the time. I'd be home with you and in your bed. Then I may never have witnessed this murder," she accused him, trying to stay calm.

He hit her across the mouth. "Don't ever talk to me like that again, you stupid bitch!"

Something broke inside her and she lost it. "I'm fucking your father, you dumb bastard," she screamed.

"What the hell are you talking about?" He stood with his arm still raised, as if to hit her again.

"You heard correctly. Since you shun me, I've looked for happiness elsewhere. I found it in your father's arms. I'm screwing him." Somehow, she found pleasure in spelling it out.

His face was an ugly mask when he looked at her. "I don't believe you. My father would never do that to me. He's a good husband to my mother and an honorable man. You're lying again, just as you lied when you accused Bakshi of murder. I can't live with you anymore. Pack you things and get the hell out of my house." He spoke with a low, monotonous and emotionless voice, like a man in a trance.

"Are you throwing me out?" Somehow she couldn't believe he'd do that.

"Get out of my sight! I've had enough of your lies and deceptions. You brought me nothing but misery. Now I have to go and try to mend things with Tanaka. I want you gone when I return." With that he stalked back to his office. Before he went

182

inside, he turned and said, "Leave your credit cards on the kitchen table."

Claire went into her bedroom and sat on her bed, wondering what just happened. Should she be happy or angry? She regretted blowing up and telling Allan about her relationship with his father. It was done and she had to live with that. Allan didn't seem to believe her, but that could change. There would be hell to pay if he confronted his father. It could ruin his marriage.

She looked around the bedroom, deciding what to take. Her laptop, for one thing. She got her suitcase out of the closet and put in some underwear, bras, a couple of dresses and other outerwear, just enough to carry her over for a few days. Anything else she could buy. Taking her credit cards out of her purse, she shrugged. It didn't matter. She had enough funds in her private bank account to last her for quite some time. Allan didn't know about that account, which meant he had no means of locking her out.

She needed a place to stay, if only for the first few days until she decided what to do next. She hoped Carmen would let her stay with her. When she called Carmen, she wasn't disappointed.

"Of course, you can stay with me. Stay as long as you want. It'll be fun." Carmen chuckled into the phone. "I'm surprised it took Allan this long to throw you out. Too bad you told him about your relationship with his father. That wasn't too smart."

"I know but it can't be changed. I only hope Aaron isn't holding it against me. I feel guilty about Elke. She's a good woman and doesn't deserve this. What makes it worse, she always treated me nice."

"I agree. That is unfortunate. The wife is always the one suffering the most when her husband takes a mistress."

"Is that what I am? Aaron's mistress?"

"How would you describe your relationship with him?"

"I never thought about that. It was never my intention to make this something permanent."

"These things never go as planned. You said Allan assumed you were just trying to get him upset. If you're lucky, he won't confront his father about it."

"I hope so. Gotta go. Still have to tie up a few things. I'll see you in a couple of hours." She was about to cut the connection when Carmen said. "Before you go, how are you fixed for money?"

"I'll be okay."

"Take my advice, load up your private account while you still can. Do it now, before Allan cuts you off."

"He'll know," Claire objected.

"What if he does? As long as you still have permission to charge on that account, he has no legal right to stop you. It's his word against yours if it ever comes to a showdown."

"I'll think about it." She put her phone on the dresser, knowing Carmen was right. This was her only chance to secure part of her future. Hoping it wasn't too late already, she opened her laptop and put in her password for the shared account. She could feel her heart beating a little faster as she waited to be signed in but it worked. The account opened. She was a bit surprised to see it contained nearly a million dollars. Allan didn't usually keep that much cash in the current account. He must be planning to pay off a large purchase. She decided she deserved at least a quarter-million dollars. Beginning to shake a little, feeling like a criminal, she initiated the process to transfer the money into her account with another bank, doing it in increments of smaller amounts. When the transfer was complete, she breathed a sigh of relief.

She tried to assure herself that she had done nothing wrong. As long as her name was on the account as a legitimate owner, she could take money from it. There was no limit on the amount she could remove. Allan should consider himself fortunate she hadn't taken everything, even though it had been tempting.

She finished packing and half an hour later she sat in her car heading for Carmen's place.

Chapter Twelve

Four days after she'd moved in with Carmen she got a call from Aaron. "Can you swing by the office today? I need to talk to you."

"What about?"

"Not on the phone. I'll tell you when you get here. It's important."

Afraid Allan told him about her blabbing what was going on between her and Aaron, she wasn't looking forward to seeing Aaron, but she couldn't dodge this one. "I'll be there shortly."

By the time she arrived at the office building, she had worked herself into a state of agitation. She steeled herself for an ugly confrontation.

"Hi, Gloria. I'm here to see my father-in-law. He's expecting me," she told the receptionist.

Gloria nodded. "I'll tell him you're here. Give me a moment." She got up and knocked on the thick oak door that gave Aaron his privacy. Opening the door, she walked into his office. She came back a couple of minutes later. "He's ready for you."

Claire gave Gloria a little smile and said, "Thank you."

Expecting the worst, completely shaken by now, she walked through the big door. Aaron stood by the window, looking out. He turned when she approached. "We have a problem."

"I'm sorry about that. I can explain."

By his expression she could tell he didn't know what she was talking about. "You can? How would you even know anything about it?"

Realizing, it must be something else he meant, she relaxed and said, "I meant perhaps I can shed some light on it once I know what the problem is."

"Remember me telling you about somebody snooping around in my computer?"

She nodded.

"Well, I suspect I know what they were after. I had a meeting with the federal agent that handles my foreign bids. I found out something quite disturbing. His department received bids on two of my upcoming contracts in Japan millions of dollars lower than mine. He told me in confidence that the bidding company is situated in the US, but it is only a shell company. The real owners live in Japan. Here is something I find suspicious. Tanaka informed me a couple of days after I had the meeting with the agent he is pulling out of our deal. He will be going with another company. I haven't found out yet which company, but I wouldn't be surprised if it is the same company that is bidding against me."

"Wow," Claire said. "I don't know what to say. I'm sorry to hear that."

"You said you may be able to explain. Do you have any ideas that may confirm my suspicion?"

"I have. Tanaka's lawyer comes to mind. I'm sure he's the man trying to blackmail us. I haven't told you this. I lured him into a hotel room, promising to pay him the ransom."

"Did you?"

"Pay him? No, but I set a trap. A friend of mine beat the crap out of him, which ended up with nasty consequences. My friend owns a horse ranch. I keep my horse there. Andy used to board his horse there, also. A couple of guys came and shot two of the horses. They also shot and wounded my friend. He killed them both while defending himself. Now he may be in trouble with the law."

Aaron looked at her with a thoughtful expression. "Do you have proof Bakshi is behind it?"

"I don't and that's the annoying part. I have nothing concrete to prove anything."

"Too bad. How can I connect him with breaking into my computer?"

"He had opportunity. Remember, he was at your birthday party?"

"I remember. So was Tanaka. Either one of them could have done it."

"Has anyone contacted you again about the ransom?"

"No, but that doesn't mean they've given up." He let out a deep sigh. "This is ugly business. I don't need this at my age." He pointed at one of the chairs. "Do you have some time? Can I get Gloria to bring you a cup of coffee?"

"That would be nice." She walked over to the chair and sank into it, relieved Aaron didn't seem to know about what happened between her and Allan.

Aaron sat down behind his desk and called Gloria on his intercom. "Bring us a couple of coffees." Then he leaned back in his chair and studied Claire. "I've missed you," he said finally.

"I've missed you, too," she said, "but the way things are right now, I think it's best if we cool it a bit until things calm down."

"You're probably right." He looked at something on his desk. "I know an FBI agent. I'm going to talk to him and see if he can find out anything about Bakshi, Tanaka, and that other company. Possibly even this cop you mentioned, what's his name…?"

"Salsky. Ron Salsky."

* * *

She was kidnapped three days later when she walked from her car to the gym. It happened so fast she didn't even have time to scream or get a good look at the van that pulled up beside her. It was black and that's all she remembered.

Two men wearing balaclavas grabbed her and pushed her into the van. Inside the van, they pulled a dark hood over her head and fastened her to the seat with the belt.

"What do you want from me?" she demanded, but nobody answered her.

As the van began to move, she gave up her struggles and sat in her seat, resigned to her fate.

When the van stopped, they dragged her out of the vehicle and into a building. She couldn't see anything through the dark material of the hood, but when they took her up two flights of stairs, she figured she was on the third floor.

They took off her hood, and she knew she was in an old, abandoned building. There was dust everywhere. The windows were filthy and covered with a layer of grime. Broken pieces of office furniture were strewn all over the floor, which was covered with fragments of old tiles.

Her abductors still had their heads and faces covered. One of them put an ankle bracelet with a lock on her left legs. It had a long chain attached to it. He locked the end of the chain around one of the old, rusted radiators on the outside wall.

Then he pointed to a pail in a corner with the words, "If you need to follow the call of nature you can use that. Don't make a mess on the floor." He spoke with a heavy eastern accent.

The other two laughed but didn't say anything.

"What about food or water?" she asked.

"Somebody will look in on you and bring you a bottle of water. As far as food goes, a couple of days without eating won't kill you. Plenty of people out there have nothing to eat."

"That's not my fault." She pulled on her chain. "What do you want from me?"

"You'll find out. Now shut up! Where is your phone?"

"In my purse." There was no use to keep it a secret. They'd find it eventually.

He picked up her purse. Rummaging around in it, he took her phone and put into his pocket. Then the three men left. She felt like screaming but knew it wouldn't do any good. The chain was barely long enough to reach to the nearest window. She had to stretch to wipe the dirt from the pane. Peering outside, she saw nothing familiar. More abandoned buildings and industrial sites. No houses, at least any see could make out through the foggy glass.

Sitting down on the floor, she contemplated her fate. She was certain it was Bakshi who was behind this. So far, her kidnappers had not harmed her, but that didn't mean they wouldn't.

The day went by without anyone coming to see her. When it got dark, she lay down on the floor and closed her eyes, hoping to get some sleep. It wasn't cold in the room, but she was shivering. Ever since she was a little girl, she never liked old places. Her rational thinking told her she was silly, but her imagination conjured up all kinds of scary things. Old buildings had their own character. The wind blowing through the empty rooms created strange sounds, the floors creaked without any living soul walking across them and the walls seemed to moan as if remembering and missing the people that once filled the now empty rooms.

She woke up once in the middle of the night to the sound of a train close by. She filed it away for future reference, but it didn't make her feel any better.

She had trouble falling asleep again, but she did. When she woke again, light fell through the windows, making the room a little less daunting. Sitting up and rubbing her eyes, she looked around the room, momentarily disoriented, but reality came back quickly.

She had been kidnapped.

When she heard the sound of footsteps coming up the stairs, she rose and watched warily, wondering who would be coming to see her.

The person she saw was the last person in the world she expected to see. Shocked and completely perplexed, she watched the woman come closer.

"Hello, Claire. I see you're up. Did you sleep well?"

"Liz?"

"Surprised to see me?" The woman laughed almost cheerfully. "Seeing the look on your face is priceless, sister-in-law. That alone is worth all the misery you've caused me these last couple of years."

"Are you still blaming me for Andy's death? It was an accident and not my fault. His horse threw him and he broke his neck."

"If it wouldn't have been for you, he would have never gone riding by himself. You lured him into your net. Probably fucked him every time you two went riding. You're a whore and a bitch." Her voice had risen and she fairly screamed the last words.

"You are wrong, Liz. Andy and I were never anything but good friends. He was my brother-in-law, for heaven's sake. Family. I would never have gotten involved with him. Neither would he with me. He loved you and I loved Allan. There was nothing going on between Andy and me. You must believe me, please."

"I don't, bitch," Liz spat. "Just because he was your brother-in-law, means nothing. You're fucking Aaron. He's your father-in-law. You seem to have no problem with that. How long has that been going on?"

"I made a mistake and I'm sorry I did. There was a reason, but you wouldn't understand. I don't understand it myself now."

Liz smirked. "Sorry doesn't cut it with me. Now you have to pay for what you did, and Aaron will pay for what he did to me."

"Is that why you had me kidnapped? To ransom me off to Aaron? Are you also involved in that blackmail scheme?"

"You got that right."

192

"I can almost understand that you hate me, even though your hate is misplaced, but why do you hate everyone else so much?"

Liz's laughter sounded shrill. "Why? You have to ask? I should have received Andy's share of the company, but what did I get?" She formed the letter O with her fingers. "This much. A big, fat zero. I didn't even get his life insurance, because the company was the beneficiary. Oh, sure, I'm getting a measly allowance every month. Just enough to live by."

Claire gave Liz a sad look. "I've never had any ill feelings toward you. I had no idea you harbored such hatred toward me and the others. Do you think you are the only one suffering after Andy's death? Allan has shunned me since that day. We haven't been intimate for two years. He hates me with a passion. Do you know he threw me out?"

"I don't care about your problems. Whatever you got you deserve," Liz hissed.

"You are the last person I expected wanting to do me harm. Of course, you're not the only one." She chuckled without humor. "If you want money from me, get in line. There is someone else trying to squeeze money out of me. I'm not paying him and I won't pay you. I don't have millions of dollars."

"I wouldn't worry about paying your friend Bakshi. He has other plans for you."

Claire stared at Liz, dumbfounded. "Are you saying you're in bed with Bakshi?"

"Not with Bakshi but with Ron Salsky. I understand you know him."

Shaking her head, confused about how this whole thing was developing, she asked, "How do you know Salsky?"

"He was the detective on the scene when Andy died, but obviously you don't remember him. He didn't have that goatee then. He's been consoling me ever since."

"Are you saying you're fucking him?"

Liz smirked. "Don't be so crude, sister-in-law. Let's put it this way—he gives me what I need."

"I feel sorry for you, Liz. You're literally in bed with some nasty people. Both those men are murderers. Don't go through with what you're planning. It will end up badly. There is still time to walk away. I won't tell anyone about you involvement. Free me and let me go," she pleaded.

"It's too late for that. I'll see this through to the end. I'm not worried about you blabbing, because you're fate is sealed. You will spend the rest of your life somewhere in Arabia, serving a sheik or some other rich Arab. I hope you'll like it."

"What are you talking about?"

"Let me tell you this, you stupid bitch---slavery is alive and well in certain parts of the world, and you will have the opportunity to find out." She blew Claire a kiss and walked away.

"You can't do this. This isn't you," Claire called, but she never looked back.

Claire looked after her with her fingers curled into fists, feeling utterly helpless and disappointed. She always liked Liz, even though they had not socialized after Andy's accident anymore. Liz had been the one pulling away from the rest of the family, but Claire never realized how she felt, never imagined she may be obsessed with such hatred toward them. Hatred that drove her to abduct Claire and wanting to sell her as a slave, condemning her to a life of misery.

Angry and desperate, she pulled on the chain that kept her prisoner, until her hands hurt.

She gave up and sat down on the floor, tears welling up inside her. This was so unfair. She had never done or wished harm to another human being. What Liz and her companions planned for her was inhumane and an unforgivable crime.

She walked again to the window, but there was nothing to see but dark clouds in the visible sky. Her view was obscured by raindrops falling against the window. It only helped to make her feel even worse. Sudden pangs of hunger did nothing to lift her spirits, either. She hadn't eaten since breakfast the day before, or had a drink of water, and she began to feel lightheaded.

When she looked at her watch, it was shortly after noon, which didn't help much. Now she was even hungrier. The worst was the silence most of the time. Only once, she heard the train again.

Footsteps on the stairs made her get up from her sitting position. Whoever it was, she wanted to look them in the eye standing up.

It didn't come as a surprise to see Bakshi. Despite her sad situation, she couldn't help but smile when she noticed him favoring his right leg.

"Did you have an accident?" she asked with a sneer.

"I'm glad you think that's funny," he said. "Enjoy that feeling, because there won't be many like that in your future."

"What are your plans for me after you get your ransom?"

"Obviously, we can't set you free. You know who we are."

"I won't tell anyone about what happened. You can have sex with me anytime you want. Perhaps it will be good. My husband doesn't have sex with me anymore. I could be your lover."

He laughed. "It sounds like a good plan, but it won't work. Eventually, you will tell."

"Liz told me something I can't believe. Are you really going to send me to Arabia or are you going to kill me in cold blood?"

"Don't worry about being killed. I'm not a murderer." He chuckled. "Well, not usually. I don't kill women. Liz told the truth about what awaits you. I will sell you as a sex slave. They say the weather is great in Yemen. You'll love it there."

"You can't just take me out of the country."

"I wouldn't worry about that. It's easier than you think. We'll get you onto the private plane of a visiting dignitary from Saudi Arabia. Nobody will ever suspect. Your husband will probably be happy to get rid of you."

"I have friends who will make inquiries."

"Don't flatter yourself, Claire. You don't have many friends. Let's see, there is Carmen." He ticked it off on his fingers. "That's one. Then we have that lawyer from Rocktown. That's two. My buddy Salsky investigated him and found something interesting. You were engaged to him at one time. We'll have to look deeper into that at a later date. Who knows what we'll discover. He might be potential prey. And then there is Randy Forrest, the guy you're fucking. Number three on the list of friends." His face darkened. "He still owes me, the bastard. I'll deal with him after this is over. As you can see, there aren't many we have to worry about. If

196

any of them think of making trouble, they will disappear."

"You forgot about my father-in-law. He knows a lot of important people."

"Oh, that's right—your father-in-law. You're fucking him, also. One of the big mistakes you made. It created a great opportunity for us. I don't doubt he knows a lot of influential people, but so do I. The secret is to know the right ones, the ones that can help you." He smiled. "You know, people disappear all the time. The cops don't have the time or the resources to bother with all of them. Besides, you're not important enough to be of interest to anyone."

"You won't get away with this. This is America. You can't kidnap people and sell them as slaves." She took a defiant stance and glared at him.

"You'd be surprised what people get away with every day in your glorious Land of the Free." He chuckled. "There is no such thing as freedom, except what the superrich that make the rules allow you. Freedom is a myth."

"I thought you were an American citizen. Am I wrong?"

"No, you're not wrong. I've been in this country for over ten years, but that doesn't mean I'll cut my ties with the country I was born."

"Where was that?"

"Saudi Arabia."

"I thought so. You're like so many of your people that come to our country. We welcome you with open arms, give you the opportunity for a great life, to live a life without fear of persecution, to practice your religion and even keep your culture. How do you repay that kindness? By creating chaos

197

and unrest, with violence and with terror. That's how."

"I haven't created any chaos or unrest. All I'm doing is taking advantage of the opportunities living in this wonderful country allow me to make money. You are correct about me not having to worry about being persecuted. As long as I'm not caught everything is alright. I don't worry about that, either. I have connections to powerful people. That's what so great about America. A man with ambitions can go places. By the way, I brought you a bottle of water. I figured you may need it by now. Sorry, I can't offer you any wine." His grin was infuriating, and his next words even more. "I haven't had the opportunity to thank you for that wonderful evening you gave me after promising me a night of passion. So I was thinking this would be a good opportunity for you to pay me back for the pain you caused me, especially since you offered it to me, anyway."

"What are you talking about?" She asked it but had no doubt about what he was planning.

He pulled a gun out of his pocket. "Get undressed."

"Why?"

"Don't act so dumb. Take off your clothes or I'll put a bullet into one of your legs." He waived his gun around.

"You don't need a gun. I'll do it, just don't hurt me."

With shaking fingers, she unbuttoned her blouse and shrugged out of it. Then she pushed down her jeans until they pooled around her ankles. Stepping out of them, she stood looking at him.

"Bra and panties. I want you naked."

She removed her bra and then her panties. Naked and shivering, she stared at him, knowing he was going to have his way with her.

"Lie down on your back and spread your legs."

She did what he wanted, closing her eyes and steeling herself to what was going to happen next.

Chapter Thirteen

She stood by the window and stared at the old buildings below. The rain had stopped during the night and it promised to be a sunny day. It did not help her mood. She felt dirty inside and outside. Bakshi had violated her body for over an hour. Before he left, he threw her a little package with the words, "I brought you a sandwich. Wouldn't want you to starve to death." He laughed as he walked away.

Her hatred for him made her almost sick. No man had ever humiliated her like that. If she had the opportunity, she would find great pleasure in putting a bullet between his eyes.

It was almost a relief when her kidnappers came up the stairs. One carried a camera and another one a stool, which he put in the middle of the room.

"Sit!"

She sat on the stool, waiting.

"We are going to make a movie," the one with the heavy accent said.

"What for?"

"You can plead with your friends to free you by paying the money we want."

"Bakshi said you won't set me free."

"It isn't up to Bakshi. We make the decisions." He pulled out a big knife and stepped behind her while the other two set up the camera.

"Why the knife?" she asked, panic-stricken.

"Don't worry. It is only for show. Look into the camera and speak when I tell you."

"Ready," one of the men behind the camera said.

"Talk," the man behind her said with a low voice.

She didn't know what to say and said the first words popping into her head. "As you see and may know by now, I've been kidnapped. Please, pay the ransom and they will set me free. I'm being held prisoner in..."

Her kidnapper put his hand over her mouth and held the knife against her throat. "If you don't pay we will send you pieces of her. We'll start with one ear, then her thumbs, then a hand until you pay. This is the only warning you will get. We will be in touch."

He made a chopping motion with his hand.

They packed up their equipment. One man handed her a bottle of water and a paper bag. "Food," he said.

The rest of the day went by slowly. She tried again to loosen the chain, but it didn't budge. When evening came, she had sunk into deep despair, wondering if Aaron would pay the ransom. Allan would not, if that she was certain. He didn't care if she lived or died.

She slept fitfully. When she slept, her dreams were disturbing, and when dawn finally came, she was tired and jittery.

Muffled voices and footsteps in the stairway prepared her for more visitors. Two of the men that had kidnapped her appeared at the top of the stairs. This time they did not have their faces and heads covered, which was not a good sign. Both were of Arabian descent and had beards.

One of them carried a bundle of what appeared to be clothing. He threw it on the floor and told her to take off her clothes.

"Are you going to rape me, too," she asked.

"You are unclean." It was the man with the heavy accent who had been talking to her before.

"Bakshi wasn't bothered by it," she said with a defiant voice.

"He is not like us. We are true believers unlike him. Now, get undressed and put these on." He pointed to the bundle on the floor.

They even made her take off her panties and bra. When she picked up the bundle from the floor, she found it to be a burka. She put it on. There was only a veil for her to see through the head covering.

"Give me your watch. You won't need it where you're going."

With reluctance, she stripped off her watch and handed it to him. "Did you get the ransom?"

"Not yet, but we will."

"You promised to let me go. This doesn't look like you are."

One of the men grabbed her arm. "We changed our mind. Let's go."

There was no sense to struggle, and she accompanied them. A black car stood waiting outside. The man pushed her into the backseat. "Put on the seatbelt," he commanded.

"Where are you taking me?"

"Does it matter if you know?"

She didn't answer. He was right, it didn't matter. Before the car started moving, she tried to remember any possible landmarks but doubted it would do her any good. There was no chance for her to escape. They were in an industrial part of the city. That's about all she could tell. Nothing looked familiar.

She stopped looking out of the window, sitting slumped in her seat, resigned to her fate. All hope of being rescued was gone.

A sound like an explosion ripped her out of her stupor. The seatbelt dug painfully into her chest as the car came to a sudden halt and was spun around, threatening to topple over. It stopped moving and she fell back into her seat.

When she looked to the front, she saw that the windshield was cracked. The man in the passenger seat sat slumped over. A few minutes later, the door was ripped open and a man asked, "Everyone alright?"

"We are fine," the driver said.

The man looked at the passenger. "He isn't. He's bleeding from a head wound. He needs to go to the hospital. I'll call an ambulance."

"He doesn't need to go to a hospital," the driver insisted, trying to start the car again, but the car didn't start.

At that moment, a cop stuck in his head. "This man is injured. How about you, sir?" He looked at the driver.

"I'm not injured."

"And you, ma'am?" He looked at Claire. "Are you okay?"

"She is," the driver said.

The cop stared at him. "I didn't ask you, sir. I asked her."

"I'm injured badly. I need to go to the hospital," Claire said, realizing this was her chance to get away.

"The lady says she's injured. Can you move or do you need help, ma'am?"

"I said she doesn't need to go to a hospital." The driver shouted. His accent was so heavy now to make his words barely comprehensible.

The cop had drawn his weapon. He aimed it at the man. "Step out of the vehicle, please."

When the driver reached into his jacket and produced a gun, the cop shot him in the head. It was unexpected and seemed unreal to Claire when the driver fell forward. The sound of the shot was loud in the confines of the car, and she realized her ordeal had come to an end with that sound.

She was free.

Stepping away from the car, the cop spoke to another person outside. Then the rear door opened and another cop looked at Claire. He held a gun in his hand. She didn't blame him for being cautious.

She lifted her hands and said, "I'm not armed if that's what you're afraid of. My name is Claire Belmont. I'm not a Muslim. These people abducted me and held me prisoner."

"Do you have any ID to prove your identity?"

Finding his question funny, she would have laughed had the situation not been so dire. "I had to leave my purse with all my papers in the old, abandoned building they kept me for these last few days."

"Take off your head covering, please, so we can see your face."

"I would if I could. It is part of this stupid garment they made me put on. I'm naked underneath."

"I understand. Are you injured in any way that will prevent you from coming out?"

"I'm not injured, only shaken up. I can move."

"Then come out of the car, please. Keep your hands where I can see them."

He stepped back but still kept his gun on her while she undid her seatbelt and slipped out.

"Keep your hands up while we frisk you." He turned to the other cop. "Check her for hidden weapons."

The other cop ran his hands over her, careful not to touch her breasts or private parts below her belly. Apparently satisfied that she had told the truth about having no gun, he stepped back. "She's clean."

"Put her into your cruiser and take her to the precinct. My partner and I will take over here."

"Alright, Serge." He took Claire's arm. "Please, come with me."

As she walked with the cop to the cruiser, she saw a few people recording everything with their phones. She was grateful to have her head and face covered, having no desire to be on the six o'clock news. She also got a glimpse of the car they had collided with. It had received substantial damage. Pieces of plastic shards lay on the street and part of the motor was exposed. Paramedics carried a person on a stretcher to the ambulance.

She took all this in with little emotion and interest. She felt drained and elated at the same time. It hadn't sunk in completely yet that she had been rescued.

The two cops in the cruiser didn't talk to her, and that was fine with her, not being in the mood to talk to anyone. All she wanted was to get home. She corrected herself. Home was with Carmen right now.

At the precinct, they signed her in and took her fingerprints at the front desk. Then one of the cops took her into a separate room with only a table and a chair on either side.

"I'll have to ask you a few questions," the cop said.

"I need to go to the washroom first. Perhaps you can find me a pair of scissors so I can cut off the head covering. I can't see much through this damned veil in front of my eyes and it drives me crazy."

"I'll call someone." He left and came back a short time later with a female cop in tow. She was big and imposing with a man's haircut. "This is Corporal Eckard. She'll take you to the washroom."

In the washroom, Claire removed the burka. Standing naked, she asked, "Did you bring scissors?"

"I did, but I can't give them to you." Eckard's expression was stony, but she couldn't completely hide her interest in Claire.

"Then do me a favor, please. Cut off the head covering." Claire handed her the burka. "Give me a few minutes. I need to clean myself. I haven't had a shower for days and I must stink like a street person. By the way, you may notice I'm not a muslin woman and I'm not hiding any weapons. So

206

give me some slack. I'm not a criminal but a victim and I want to go home as soon as possible."

"And you will, as soon as we have established your identity."

Claire pulled off a few sheets of the paper towels, made them wet, and rubbed down her body, especially her genital area, not caring if the cop watched or not. Then she washed her face and gargled with water.

"I wish I had descent clothes to put on." She sighed. "I guess I'll have to wear this demeaning outfit until I get home." She pulled the burka over her head and looked at herself in the mirror. "I look awful. My hair is a mess. I need to put on makeup. Let's get this over with."

"Like I said, we need to establish your identity first and go over a few questions. Then you'll be free to go."

She accompanied Claire back to the interrogation room. "Please, take your seat again. Someone will be with you in a moment." Then she left.

A few moments later another woman came into the room. She didn't wear a uniform. She sat down in the chair across from Claire, put her phone on the table and introduced herself. "I'm Detective Morgan. We thought you might be more relaxed talking to a woman. My information tells me you claim to have been kidnapped."

"It's not a claim. It's the truth. I was kidnapped four days ago in the parking lot of the gym I frequent by three men wearing balaclavas. They grabbed me after I left my car and shoved me into a van. They took me to an abandoned warehouse

207

somewhere in an industrial area of the city, where I was kept until today. I was starved, videotaped and raped. This morning, they put me into a car to take me to the airport, where I would have been forced to board the private plane of a visiting dignitary from Saudi Arabia. I was going to be sold to some Sheik to join his harem. As a sex-slave."

"That's quite some story," the detective commented.

Claire bent forward, feeling annoyed and frustrated. "No story. Perhaps you should get a piece of paper and write everything down. My name is Claire Belmont. I'm married to Allan Belmont. He owns Belmont Advertising. My father-in-law is Aaron Belmont, CEO of KOBOLD Engineering Construction Corp, USA. To substantiate my claim I was abducted, my car is probably still in the parking lot of Get Fit Today."

"I don't need to write it down, Missis Belmont. I have an excellent memory. Besides, everything you say is recorded by my cellphone. Before we go any further, I should advise you that you don't have to tell me anything without the presence of your lawyer. Should you prefer that option, you will have to stay in custody until your lawyer arrives."

"I don't need a lawyer, because I haven't done anything wrong. I'm the victim here. I was kidnapped."

Detective Morgan nodded. "Okay then. Can you give me the location of this warehouse?"

"No. There was a train nearby, that's all I know."

"That's not much to go on. What happened to your clothes and your identification papers?"

"My driver's licence, credit cards and other papers that would identify me are in my purse, which is back in that warehouse, along with my clothes."

"You claim to have been raped."

"Like I said before, I'm not claiming anything. Everything I'm telling you is the truth. When I say I was raped it means I was raped." Claire was getting impatient and infuriated. "Listen, can we stop playing 'A thousand questions' and get down to the important stuff."

Morgan gave her a tight smile. "No need to get offensive. I'm only doing my job, which is to identify who you are. To me you are a stranger in a burka. You were in the company of two Muslim men. You have no papers. It is not up to me to prove your identity. That is your job. I have no way of knowing if you're a Muslim woman or not, or that you aren't a member of some Islamic terror group."

"Well, I can assure you I'm not."

"I only have your word. Unless you can prove who you really are, I have to treat you with suspicion. Can you identify the men that abducted and raped you?"

"I've never seen the men that abducted me before, but I can tell you who's behind my abduction and the name of the man who raped me."

"Are you saying more people besides the three abductors were involved?" Morgan looked at her sharply. "How do you know this?"

"Because I know them. The name of the man who raped me is Mohan Bakshi. He is a lawyer and

209

he works for a Mister Kaito Tanaka, an international shoe manufacturer."

"Let me stop you right there. You said you know this man. How?"

"I saw him murder a drug dealer by the name of Joe Moretti. Him and Ron Salsky, who incidentally is a cop." She paused to let that sink in.

Morgan lifted both hands. "Woah, hold it right there. This is getting more and more complicated. Drug dealers and a murder. Now you're telling me a member of the police force is involved. Can you prove that?"

"I reported all of it to the DA's office. I have no idea what they did with that information."

"Let's leave it at that for the moment. I can easily check it out. You mentioned another person. I can't wait to find out who that could be."

Her flippant comment irked Claire. "I can see you don't believe me. I know, this all seems weird, but it is the truth. The person who masterminded my kidnapping is my sister-in-law Liz Belmont."

"Your sister-in-law? Interesting. What reason would she have to kidnap you?" Morgan made no effort to hide her skepticism.

"She blames me for her husband's death. His name was Andy Belmont. He was thrown by his horse and broke his neck. The accident happened two years ago. You should have no problem checking that out, also. It probably is somewhere in the police reports." She folded her hands and stared at the table top. "I'm getting tired. I just want to go home."

"You will, as soon as we identify you as the person you claim to be."

210

"You like to use the word claim, don't you?" Claire's patience was at a low point. "All you have to do is call my husband. He will verify my identity."

Detective Morgan dialed the number Claire gave her. She hoped he would answer.

"Am I speaking to Mister Allan Belmont?" After a short pause, she said, "This is Detective Morgan from the 34th precinct. We have a woman in custody who claims she is Missis Claire Morgan. Apparently, she had been kidnapped, but she escaped. Can you verify that claim?"

Another short pause.

Morgan looked at Claire as she spoke into her phone. "Interesting. You say you weren't aware of her being kidnapped. Has your wife been missing for these last few days? You don't know that, either?"

She paused again, listening. "Tell me, Mister Belmont. Is there actually a Missis Belmont?"

After putting the phone back onto the table, she gave Claire a long look. "He says as far as he is concerned, you don't exist. What am I to make out of that?"

"I'm not surprised he said that. In fact, I expected as much. Our marriage is finished. I moved out a week ago." She lifted her face and stared at the ceiling for a moment, silently cursing Allan. "Call my father-in-law. He will not deny me." She gave the detective Aaron's private number.

Morgan got up and turned away when she spoke to Aaron. When she looked at Claire again, she said, "He said he is sending a car to pick you up. It seems to me he really cares about you. He told me he is relieved to hear you're unharmed."

"He's a good man," Claire said. "Unlike his son."

Chapter Fourteen

When the driver picked her up at the police station, he told her he had orders from his boss to take her to her home. "Mister Belmont said it's your home as well as Allan's. You have to stand up for your rights."

"That's easy to say. My husband will throw me out again, but that's okay. Tomorrow, I'll move back in with my girlfriend. She'll be happy to see me. Right now, I'm too tired to worry what Allan will do."

He wasn't at home and she thanked her lucky stars. Carol was there doing some cleaning. At first, she didn't recognize Claire in her burka, but when she did, she gave her a concerned smile. "I'm so happy to see you, but what happened to you, Missis Belmont?"

"I had a run-in with some nasty people. I'll tell you a little bit about it later, but the first thing I need to do is take a long bath and get into some descent clothes. After that, I'd like to eat something. I haven't eaten a decent meal for days. Perhaps, you can throw something together for me. Also, get me a bottle of wine."

"No problem, Missis Belmont. Do you want me to draw you the bath?"

"Not necessary. I can to that myself."

After fairly ripping the hated garment off her body, she looked at herself in the mirror and smiled at her image. "I may have lost a couple of pounds. There are good sides to everything."

She threw the burka into the garbage can, glad to be rid of it. 'How women are willing to wear this every day is beyond me. I wouldn't want any of my friends to see me in an outfit like that. It's demeaning.'

Lying in the tub, her body submerged in warm water, made her feel drowsy, but she fought to stay awake. It would be ironic to drown in a tub after escaping from a nearly terrible fate.

Carol had made her an omelette and fried up some potatoes. "There isn't much in the fridge," she said with an apologizing gesture. "Mister Belmont hardly eats at home anymore."

"When do you expect him home?"

Carol shrugged. "He didn't tell me. I never know when he comes home. He may be early or very late. Ever since you left, I've been staying here every day. Mister Belmont said he feels better if someone is in the house when he's not here. I usually start at seven to make breakfast for him and leave at around four. Most of the time, he hasn't come home yet when I leave. Sorry, I can't give you more information."

"That's okay." She looked at the clock on the stove. "You should be going home. It's almost five."

"Will you be staying from now on, Missis Belmont?"

"I don't think so. My husband and I had a big fight and he threw me out of the house. Unless he changed his mind, which I doubt, I'll be gone in a couple of days. Listen, do me a favor and don't come for the next few days until things have settled down. I'll let you know when it's okay to come back."

"Are you sure about that? I wouldn't want Mister Belmont getting mad at me. I need this job."

"Don't worry about it. I'll tell him I gave you the week off."

Carrol rushed up to her and touched her hand with a quick gesture. "Thank you, Missis Belmont. You've always been so kind. You're a good person. I hope you can mend things with Mister Belmont." She giggled. "My boyfriend will be happy. This will be an occasion to spend more time with him. He's been complaining. Men can be such little boys sometimes."

"Go and enjoy his company. Live every day as if it's your last with him, but don't let him take advantage of you. You'll be much happier. Now, go."

Allan came home late in the evening. When he saw Claire, his scowled and said, "I didn't invite you back into the house."

"It was your father's idea. He says this house is as much mine as it is yours."

"Well, he's wrong."

"Aren't you at least interested what happened to me?"

"Actually not, but I'm sure you will enlighten me." He walked to the liqueur cabinet, took out a bottle and poured himself a drink. Then he reached for the newspaper, which she had put onto the table.

"Are you really so callous, Allan? Even if you don't love me anymore, there has to be at least a shred of curiosity in you. I'm not an object you can discard like a useless piece of tool you don't need anymore. I'm your wife. I'm someone you once loved and who loved you."

"You said it. Once. It seems an eternity ago. I have no feelings left for you, Claire. Face it and accept it."

She heaved a deep sigh. "I've accepted it a long time ago, but I still care enough to warn you against certain people you trust. I know you don't believe me anymore, but for once I wish you would take what I tell you seriously. I don't know if you and Tanaka are back in business. For your sake I hope not. I have a bad feeling things will not end up well. It was his lawyer, Mohan Bakshi, who was behind my kidnapping. He also raped me, in case you care. You are aware that I was kidnapped, right? The police advised you of it. Bakshi didn't act alone. His buddy, Ron Salsky, was also involved, but the real mastermind behind the whole thing was your sister-in-law, Liz."

He had only been half-listening to her, pretending to be busy reading the paper, but that got his attention. He actually broke into loud laughter. "Now I know you are nuts. What reason would Liz have to even think about a crazy scheme like that?"

"Many reasons. She hates me because, according to her, it was my fault Andy died, but she hates you and your father even more for not giving her Andy's share of the company."

"What? She was never interested in the business. Besides, my father is paying her a generous allowance, more than enough for her to be financially comfortable."

"Not according to her. She is bitter, consumed by hatred and rage, and she wants revenge.

Did your father tell you that he is being blackmailed? They want two million dollars from him."

"For what?"

"He wants to keep that a secret and it's not important. Liz and Bakshi are behind that. Just ask him and he will confirm it."

"I will, but first I'm going to call Liz and tell her about your absurd accusation. I'm sure she'll get a good laugh first and then she'll sue you for slander."

"Go ahead and call her, but be advised if you do that we'll both be dead. She is involved with some nasty people."

"You mean with Bakshi and Salsky? Bakshi is a lawyer and Salsky is a cop."

"Yes, they are, and that makes them a couple of stand-up citizens in your eyes? Let me remind you. They already committed one murder, but you didn't believe me about that, either."

"I don't believe anything you say, anymore. You're a whore and a liar. You claimed to have sex with my father, you caused my brother's death, and now you accuse my sister-in-law of this terrible crime. What have you planned for my sister and me?"

"Andy's death was an accident and you can't blame me for that, even though you've punished me for it all these years."

"I'm going to put this accusation about Liz to rest right now." He picked up his cell and said, "Call Liz Belmont."

Liz answered the call almost immediately. "What can I do for you, Allan?"

217

"Hi Liz. This is almost embarrassing, but I had to call you about it. I know you'll get a good laugh. Claire came home and she claims she's been kidnapped. It may be true or not, but this is the part that makes me question her sanity. She says you are behind the kidnapping. I don't believe it, of course, but I'd like to hear your comment."

Liz actually laughed. It sounded shrilly over the phone. "I'm glad to hear you say you don't believe her. That is the most ridiculous thing I ever heard in my life. You have good reason to question her mental state. Obviously, she's gone insane. She may even be dangerous. I'd fear for my life if I were you. You should have her committed."

"Another question. Do you know a cop by then name of Ron Salsky?"

"Never heard of him. Why?"

"Something else Claire mentioned. I'm glad I talked to you. Don't worry. What we talked about stays between us. Don't mention it to anyone else, please. You only confirmed what I suspected all along. Talk to you. Take care."

He gave Claire a thoughtful look after he put the phone down. There was pity in his voice when he spoke. "You heard. What am I going to do with you? I don't believe you have it in you to harm me or others, but I think you should get professional help. I know a good psychiatrist. He can be trusted. I'm going to set up an appointment. I'll even go with you to introduce you."

"I'm not crazy, Allan, but you are right about one thing…you have nothing to fear from me. It is Liz you have to worry about. She, Salsky, and Bakshi are the danger. They are ruthless and will

218

not shy away from murdering you and me, especially now that I'm free again. I am a threat, and they will come for me, and now for you. I advise you to hire a couple of guards."

Allan filled another shot-glass, careful not to spill anything. Then he stared at it, as if debating about actually drinking it. Shrugging, he downed it, put the glass on the table and pressed the cork back into the bottle. Then he lifted his gaze and studied Claire. "I feel sorry for you, Claire. You've changed these past two years. You used to be warm and understanding, never took part in gossip, never talked negatively about anyone. That's what I admired about you. I don't know what happened to you. This paranoia is not normal."

"You don't believe I was kidnapped?"

"I don't know what to believe."

"All you have to do is call the precinct where I was kept and interrogated. The car that was going to take me to the airport was involved in an accident. That's how I escaped my captors, otherwise I would have ended up in an airplane flying to Saudi Arabia to be sold as a sex-slave."

"Claire, Claire. Do you hear yourself? Is there no end to your imagination? A sex-slave in Saudi Arabia? That is almost sick. Where do you come up with this stuff?"

"Perhaps if you would have been interested in what Detective Morgan had to tell you, you would have known that. Call her and find out the truth."

"I don't even know who this Detective Morgan is. Is she a real person?"

"I have her card. All you have to do is pick up the phone and give her a call. Perhaps you'll change your mind about my story."

He made a dismissing motion. "Maybe I'll call her tomorrow. If she actually exists. Right now, I'm tired. I had a tough day. The last thing I needed today was to find you here and listen to that fantastic story of yours. It's getting late, I'm going to bed." He got up and left.

She went to her own bedroom, suddenly quite tired. Before she got ready for bed, she called Carmen.

From Carmen's reaction, she knew her girlfriend had been worried about her. "Where are you calling from?"

"From my home. I mean, Allan's place."

"Are you two back together again?"

"No. This is just temporary."

"Where have you been?"

"Rotting in some abandoned warehouse. I was kidnapped."

There was a pause on the other end. Obviously, Carmen was trying to make sense of what Claire told her. When she spoke again, she said, "Kidnapped? Who would want to kidnap you?"

"My old friend Bakshi, but the person really behind it all is my sister-in-law, Liz. It's a long story. I can't tell you over the phone. I just wanted you to know that I'm safe…for now."

"What do you mean by for now?"

"I'm afraid they'll be coming for me. If anything happens to me, call a Detective Morgan at the 34th Precinct and tell her what we saw that day by the lake. Also, call Randy and tell him I love him

220

and I'm sorry to have dragged him into this. Tell him to call Roy. He will need a good lawyer. I may need one also...if I'm still alive. I'll text you all the information. I will also email you more detailed stuff about what happened to me. Can you do this for me, please?"

"You're scaring me. What do you expect will happen?"

"I don't know. I hope nothing in the next little while. Hopefully, I'll see you soon and I can tell you everything in person. I love you, Carmen. You've been a good friend." After she hung up, she sent a text message, giving her names and phone numbers. Then she sent the email, describing how she was kidnapped and who was behind her kidnapping, hoping Carmen wouldn't have to follow up on anything.

She was surprised to find Allan still home in the morning.

"I'm giving you the benefit of the doubt, Claire. I will call that detective and find out more details about what you told me."

"I appreciate that, Allan. I would never make up a story like that. What would be the point?"

"I don't know." He looked up when the phone in the kitchen rang. "Who could that be? Are you expecting any calls?"

"No. Anyone calling me would do so on my cell. Maybe it's one of those annoying sales calls."

When the phone didn't stop ringing, she went and picked it up. "Belmont residence."

"Is Mister Belmont in?"

"Who shall I say is calling?"

"This is Mister Tanaka's office. Mister Tanaka says it is important Mister Belmont and he meet. He has sent a car to pick up Mister Belmont to take him to a private place. This meeting has to be made in secret. Mister Tanaka will explain everything to Mister Belmont in person. The car should be at your residence by now. Is Mister Belmont there?"

"Just a moment. I will find out." She covered up the mouthpiece of the phone and said, "It's Tanaka's office. He wants a meeting with you. The driver will pick you up in a few minutes. What do you want to do?"

"Give me the phone." He took it out of Claire's hand and said into the speaker, "Belmont here. What is this all about?" After listening to the caller, he said, "Alright. I'll meet with Mister Tanaka." He put down the phone. "I wonder what he wants."

The doorbell rang a few minutes later.

"Please, get it. I want to talk to the driver first. Send him to my office."

Claire went to the front door and opened it. The two men that forced their way past her into the house had their faces and heads covered. One of them grabbed Claire. Her scream to warn Allan was cut short when he put his hand over her mouth. Allan came out of his office to see what happened. He jumped back into his office when he saw the two masked intruders but too late. The other man had reached him, grabbed him by the collar and dragged him out.

Allan shook off his hands. "If you want to rob me, I don't have any cash in the house, except for the few dollars I carry in my wallet." Allan sounded

222

belligerent, obviously not seeing the danger Claire knew they were facing.

"We don't want your money," the one holding her said.

She froze. She recognized that voice. It belonged to one of her kidnappers, the one that hadn't been in the car when they drove to the airport.

"What do you want if you're not after money?"

Claire struggled in her captor's grip. "They're going to kill us, Allan. I warned you, but you didn't believe me."

"Stop being so melodramatic. They won't gain anything by killing us," Allan said. Then he addressed the intruders, "If you'll tell me what this is all about, perhaps we can come to an agreement. Did Mister Tanaka send you?"

"Actually, Mister Tanaka has nothing to do with this. Mister Bakshi sends his regards," the man standing near him said.

"Mister Bakshi? What does he want from me?"

"Nothing from you. His grievance is with your wife. He isn't happy with her at all." He looked at Claire. "You were lucky when that accident happened, but if you think you got away, you're wrong."

Claire tried to free herself. "Whatever you're planning, you won't get away with it. By now the police probably interrogated your friend in the hospital and they know everything about Bakshi."

"You'll be disappointed to hear that the police got nothing. One of the two men that were supposed to take you to the plane was shot to death, but you know that, and the other one succumbed to his injuries in the hospital."

"I told the police everything," she said in desperation.

"They have only your word but nothing to prove anything. Remember, Mister Bakshi is a lawyer. He has many friends in the police department."

"I know one of his friends. He is a murderer, as is Bakshi. Killing me will be the final nail in both their coffins. I have friends that won't rest until those two are brought to justice." She tried again to get free, without success.

"Don't worry, we won't kill you. What Mister Bakshi has planned for you is worse than your fate would have been in Yemen. We're going to kill your husband, instead." He pulled out a knife and before Allan could react, the man stabbed him in the chest.

Allan staggered and collapsed.

Claire wanted to scream, but no sound escaped her mouth. She watched in horror as the man stabbed Allan repeatedly in the back. Then he got up, strolled casually to the cupboard and removed a large frying pan. Walking back to where Allan lay in a pool of blood, he smashed the frying pan against Allan's head a couple of times.

Standing over Allan lifeless body, he said, "That should do it."

A sob escaped Claire's mouth. She had hated Allan for the way he treated her, but not so much to want him dead, murdered in such horrible fashion. He didn't deserve that. "You're not a human being but a monster," she screamed. "He did nothing to you. May you rot in hell! You'll pay for this."

Laughing over her outburst, the man said, "Not me. You will pay for the murder of your husband."

She felt a prick in her neck and everything went dark.

Chapter Fifteen

Feeling disoriented for a moment, she stared at the ceiling. Memory flooded back like a rushing waterfall. Sitting up, she looked around, searching for Allan's body. He lay not far away. Rising to her feet, she felt something in her hand. She looked and saw the bloody knife. Throwing it away, she began to rise but stopped when she heard someone speak.

"I never knew you hated Allan enough to murder him," a familiar voice said.

She got up and stood on wobbly legs, staring at Liz who sat in one of the kitchen chairs. "I didn't kill him, but I'm sure you know that."

"I know it and you know it, but the people looking at the evidence don't. I took a bunch of pictures while you lay with the bloody knife you used to stab Allan in your hand. Pictures don't lie." Her laughter sounded like the cackling of a wicked witch.

Claire couldn't believe this was the same woman she played tennis with when Andy was still alive. "What happened to you, Liz? You and I were never close friends, but we shared good times together. Now you've turned into this evil person that I don't know. Your hatred will be your undoing."

"Don't worry about me, dear sister-in-law. You will finally get what you had coming to you."

"Nobody will believe I killed Allan. Whatever pictures you took of me won't stand up in court. I'm going to wash up now and then I'll call my lawyer."

"I don't think so. You just stay put where you are." Liz pulled a gun out of her purse and waived it around. "Perhaps I should shoot you in the legs. I'm a good shot. I won't miss."

"Why are you doing this, Liz?"

"You know why, bitch. You always pretended to be this good, loving person. I know that you were Aaron's favorite. He never liked me. I have no idea why, but I can guess. He had the hots for you all along and you will spread your legs for any male that asks. You let Bakshi fuck you after you fucked Allan's cousin Charles." She chuckled. "I guess you had no idea I know about that. Bakshi told me all about it. Now you're giving it to Aaron, your own father-in-law. You're a sick person. Don't you have any shame? I also know about Randy Forest. How many other guys are there? I'm sure there are more. No wonder Allan finally threw you out of the house."

"My sex-life is none of your business."

"It is if I can use it to my advantage. I'm going to enjoy showing the pictures of you and Aaron to the judge. That'll convince him and the jury of your guilt. You needed to get Allan out of the way to be free for Aaron. You will fry for murdering Allan, no matter what you tell them. Who will believe you?" She tilted her head to listen. "I believe the police have arrived."

Claire felt sudden despair. There was no way out of this one. The evidence was stacked against her, especially if Liz took pictures of her holding the knife. She couldn't rely on surveillance cameras to tell the real story, because there weren't any. Allan didn't want any in the house. Her only hope was the camera outside. It might show the two men that murdered Allan as they approached the house.

Her heart sank when the two cops walked in. One of them was Ron Salsky.

Liz acted as if she didn't know him. "I'm so glad you came so fast, officers," she said, addressing the cop with Salsky. "I am Liz Cameron, the deceased's sister-in-law. I came this morning to see how things were going, since Claire, my brother-in-law's wife, hadn't been home for days. He was worried something may have happened to her. I spoke to him a few days ago, and he told me Claire had not been well for quite some time, suffering from some kind of paranoia. She began hallucinating, seeing things, and accusing people of wanting to kill her. She even accused me, but I don't want to get into that now. When I entered the house, I found Allan lying in a pool of blood on the floor. I knew immediately he was dead. Then I saw Claire lying not far from him, unconscious, with the bloody knife in her hand. I took pictures to prove it." She sniffed and wiped her eyes. "This is terrible. Why would she murder her own husband? He was a good man, you know."

Salsky walked up to her and stroked her shoulder. "Calm down, Missis Belmont. We'll sort all this out. Have you touched anything?"

"No, I haven't. Claire, of course, threw away the knife, but that is understandable. I probably would have done the same thing."

"May I see the pictures?"

Liz handed him her phone. "I know they are evidence, but can you transfer them to your phone?

228

I have a lot of private stuff on mine and I don't want to give it up."

"No problem." Salsky turned to his partner. "Langdon, I'll let you arrest her. Her name is Claire Belmont. You know the procedure."

The other cop approached Claire. She watched him coming closer, filled with despair.

"I didn't do it," she said with a low voice. "Two men wearing balaclavas murdered him."

"You can tell that to the judge. Missis Claire Belmont, you are under arrest for the murder of your husband Allan Belmont. You have the right to remain silent. Anything you say...."

She didn't listen, just stood there, dazed and dumbfounded. The whole situation seemed unreal. She felt like a person in a dream, watching a scene unfold. This wasn't her. This couldn't happen to her, not in real life. Any moment she would wake up from this nightmare. That's all it was...a nightmare.

They allowed her one phone call. She called Carmen.

"Carmen, this is Claire. Listen carefully. Don't say anything, just listen. Two masked men came into our house this morning and they murdered Allan. I've been arrested for his murder and right now I'm in jail. I'm being framed by the people I mentioned in my email. Please, follow the instructions I sent you. Do it immediately. Tell them about me being arrested and why. Also call my father-in-law. His private number is with the information in my email. Make it clear to him that I did not murder Allan. Then drive out to Randy's place, show him my email, and ask him if you can stay with him. You may not be safe, either. Do all this still today, please."

She didn't wait for Carmen to comment before she hung up.

Back in her cell, she sat on her bunk, contemplating life and the universe. She was not religious, but she believed in a higher power, some universal force controlling all life. She didn't believe that a person's life was mapped out when they were born. There had to be more to it, otherwise what was the point in living, if every person was nothing but a puppet, an actor on a giant stage? She had always believed in a certain amount of free will. People were given choices; they were given opportunities to choose the road they wanted to take as they moved through time until they reached the end of their life.

Where had she gone wrong? At what point in her life did she choose the wrong road? Some people believed in reincarnation. They believed that a soul planned its life already before they were born. Somehow, she couldn't believe she would have chosen a life of misery, a life where she may spend the rest of her life rotting in a jail cell.

Did she choose the wrong road as a teenager when she decided to sell her body as a sex-object to a bunch of old, horny men? Or was it her decision to leave Rocktown and Roy? Had she married Roy, she wouldn't be sitting in this cell right now. Perhaps, she made the wrong choice when she married Allan. Maybe it was her fault he was dead now. Maybe she caused the death of Andy. Had

230

they not gone riding that fateful day, he may be alive today.

Every decision one makes, carries consequences. Was every decision she made the wrong one? If there was such an omnipotent force, wasn't it possible she was punished for all the bad decisions she made in her life.

Somehow, that wasn't something she was willing to accept.

She pressed her hands against her head, trying to force those dark thoughts out of her mind. There was no purpose in torturing herself. It wouldn't change a thing. She was not an evil person. She was not the perpetrator here but the victim, and she would fight to the end to prove her innocence and make sure the guilty ones were punished.

The next four days went by without any visits or phone calls and she was afraid her friends had abandoned her.

On the fifth day she had a visitor.

Separated by a sheet of glass, not being able to touch another living person when she needed to be held and comforted, was pure agony. She picked up the phone with a shaking hand. Her voice sounded strange in her ears. "Hi Randy. You're my first ray of sunshine ever since they stuck me into this dungeon."

"I'm sorry it took so long to visit you, but they wouldn't let me see you. They told me only family and your lawyer would be allowed to talk to you."

She put her hand flat against the glass. When he put his on the other side, a sob escaped her lips. "I wish I could feel you. I feel so alone and lost. I've missed you."

"I miss you, too. Carmen told me everything about your abduction. I feel miserable I wasn't able to help you. I didn't know."

"Is Carmen with you?"

"She is. I hired the services of a private protection company. They sent a couple of armed guards to the ranch. She should be safe. I contacted Roy Sanders, the attorney you told me about. He will be coming to visit you tomorrow. He sounds like a nice guy. How do you know him?"

"You may remember me telling you I grew up in Rocktown. Roy and I are old friends."

"I got the feeling there was more to your relationship with him."

She sighed. "There was. I was engaged to Roy, but that was a long time ago. Now we're just good friends. He is the only lawyer I trust. He would not betray me."

"Good. I want to make sure you are represented by someone who has your best interest at heart."

"He has. There are not many people I trust these days."

He smiled. "I hope you trust me."

"With my life. I've had plenty of opportunity these past days to think about my life and the people in it. I realized that I love you. If there is one person I'd have to choose to spend the rest of my life with it would be you."

"I love you, too, Claire. I will leave no stone unturned to prove your innocence. Don't lose hope. We'll beat this. You have the best team in the world on your side."

Before she could respond, the guard came and grabbed the phone from of her hand. "Time's up."

She blew Randy a kiss as the guard took her away, her mood in a more positive state. She would win this. This was not the end of her life.

The next day, the guard came and led her into a separate room. He told her to sit in one of the chairs at the table in the center of the room. "Your lawyer is here. You have one hour to tell him your story. No touching or accepting anything. Any violation, and the interview is over. Remember that."

When Roy walked in she was surprised to see Sylvia Preston with him.

"Hi, Roy. I see you brought company."

Roy seemed embarrassed and somewhat awkward. "Yes, I have. You remember Sylvia?"

"I do. I saw her last at Evelyn's funeral." She looked at Sylvia. "I have to admit, you're the last person I expected."

Sylvia moved her fingers in a small wave. "Hi, Claire. I convinced Roy to take me with him. You know, mix pleasure with business. We both needed to get away." Her expression was one of concern. "I hope you make it out of here. You sure got a bad rap, but Roy is a good lawyer."

"I hope he is. I need the best. My situation looks hopeless. Everything points to my guilt." Her eyes focused on Roy. "Is Sylvia your secretary or something?"

Sylvia laughed and answered her question, "Oh no. I don't know anything about the law. Roy and I are merely two lonely people who were looking for companionship. It just happened." She touched Roy's arm. "Right, honey."

He gave Claire a sheepish look. "She was there when I needed someone to comfort me."

233

"I see." Claire swallowed and shrugged. "I'm happy for you both. Now, let's get to the real reason you're here."

He sat down in the chair facing Claire, took his phone out of his pocket and put it onto the table. "Tell me everything you can remember. Even stuff you may think is not important. Every little bit helps me to make a case. Whatever you say stays between you and me."

"And Sylvia," Claire said.

Roy turned to Sylvia. "Sorry, you will have to leave the room."

She bent down and kissed him on the cheek. "That's okay. There is no place for me to sit, anyway."

Claire was happy to see her walk out of the door. When Sylvia was outside, Roy didn't say anything for a while, pretending to be busy fiddling with his phone. When he looked up, his expression was one of sorrow. "I didn't plan for that to happen, Claire. My feelings for you haven't changed. I still love you, but it wouldn't have worked out. You were a married woman, and now…" He shook his head, folded his hands and stared at the table top. "Whatever I say will be the wrong thing."

"Then let me say it for you. Now I'm accused of murdering my husband. It would not have looked good should there have been some romantic connection between you and me. Perhaps this will be for the best. I need you as my lawyer not my lover."

He pursed his lips. "I'm glad you feel that way. Then let's begin."

"She looked at the clock on the wall. "I only have one hour, of which we already wasted almost ten minutes. So I have to make it quick. It all started on the day my brother-in-law died…"

Roy had been sitting silent the whole time, but she knew he had listened carefully. She couldn't tell from his expression what he thought. Except when he spoke, he betrayed his emotion. "There is one thing I don't understand. Why would you have sex with your father-in-law?"

She couldn't stop the sudden tears in her eyes. "I made a horrible mistake and now I pay for it. Allan paid for it with his life. Without those pictures, they would have nothing on me or Aaron."

"You said it was your girlfriend's idea. How much to you trust her?"

"Carmen? I hope you're not suggesting she may be behind the ransom attempt?"

"I'm playing with it in my mind. Your sister-in-law, Liz, already betrayed you. That came as a complete surprise. It is strange sometimes how little we know about even our close friends."

Claire shook her head vehemently. "Not Carmen. I trust her with my life. She doesn't need to think of schemes to make money. She has more than she ever needs."

He lifted his hands. "Just an idea. I'm not accusing her. You said you had sex with this Bakshi in your father-in-law's office. That means he had access to that computer. You may have to testify to that in court. Are you willing to do that?"

"Whatever I need to do to gain back my freedom. After this, my reputation is shot to hell anyway. I only ask to keep my affair with Aaron out of it. I don't want to ruin his marriage."

"I will bring it up only with your permission. We'll save that for the event we may run into a brick wall. So far, I don't see it as being imperative to your case. It may even be taken as a stumbling block. There is the problem though it may be revealed by Liz. She seems like a vindictive woman who is out to destroy you and Aaron Belmont. I have no control over that. If she is put on the witness stand, she will bring it up."

"Not necessarily, because admitting her knowledge about me and Aaron will implicate her in the ransom attempt. There is no way for her to know about the pictures, unless she is involved. She will deny her relationship with Ron Salsky and Bakshi. One more thing. Contact Detective Morgan at the 34th precinct and find out if they made any headway in my case. I told her most of the stuff I told you, not everything, though, so be careful what you reveal. I left out the more personal details. Also, get in touch with my father-in-law and see how the investigation with the ransom is going. He has connections you may be able to take advantage of." She looked at the clock. "We only have a few minutes left. Did you speak to Randy already?"

"Yes, I have. I got the feeling he cares for you. He seems like a good man."

"He is." She felt like giving him a hug, but she knew they were being watched. "I wish it would have worked out differently for us," she said with a subdued voice. "I'm glad you found someone you can share your grief with."

236

"Thank you." He hesitated. "We may not see each other till the trial. I promise I will do my best to get you out. Take care, Claire." He got up and walked away.

She waited for the guard to take her back to her cell. Somehow, she felt empty inside with little hope to ever taste freedom again.

237

Chapter Sixteen

She lost track of time. The days in prison turned into an endless procession of boredom and despair. When the day of her trial came, it seemed unreal, almost unexpected.

She was surprised at the number of people in the courtroom. Randy was there. Carmen sat beside him. She gave Claire a little wave and smiled encouragingly. She didn't see Aaron.

The guard took her to her place. She sat down, wondering where Roy was, but she needn't have worried. He walked in a few minutes later. Sylvia was with him, but she took her seat on one of the benches.

Roy joined Claire and sat down beside her. He reached for her hand and held it for a moment. "Everything will be alright," he said. "Don't worry. Just stick to the truth. There is the bailiff."

Claire nodded, not feeling confident. When the bailiff said, "Order in the Court," she realized her trial was about to begin, and when the judge walked in and took his seat behind the bench, she knew this was it.

The bailiff spoke again. "All rise. The Court of the Second Judicial Circuit, Criminal Division, is now in session, the Honorable Judge Jeremy Milner presiding."

She rose with everyone else and stood with shaking knees, wondering if Judge Milner was a fair judge.

"Everyone but the jury may be seated. Mister Sinclair, please swear in the jury."

Judge Milner waited until the bailiff told the jurors to lift their right hand and swear to listen to the case and render a fair verdict. Then he looked around the courtroom. "Good morning, ladies and gentlemen. Calling the case of the People of the State of Colorado versus Claire Belmont. Is the prosecution ready?"

The prosecuting attorney stood up. "Ready for the People, your Honor."

"Is the defence ready?"

This time Roy rose and said, "Yes, your Honor."

Then she heard the prosecutor again. "Your Honor and ladies and gentlemen of the jury, my name is William Stenton. I am representing the State of Colorado and I will prove to you without the shadow of a doubt that Missis Claire Belmont murdered her husband, Allan Belmont, in cold blood. She stabbed him more than a dozen times. When he lay in a pool of his own blood on the floor, she viciously bashed in his head with a cast iron frying pan. Please, find the defendant guilty. Thank you."

Roy stood up. "Your Honor, members of the Jury. My name is Roy Sanders. I am representing the accused, Missis Claire Belmont. I intend to prove to you that Missis Belmont is innocent of the crime. She did not murder her husband but was framed. I also intend to provide this court and the jury with the names of the people behind it. After viewing the evidence I will provide, I ask the court

239

and the jury to find the defendant not guilty. Thank you."

He sat down and pulled out a notebook from his case.

The judge spoke again. "Prosecution, you may call your first witness."

"Thank you, your Honor. I call to the stand Missis Elizabeth Belmont."

"Will the witness please stand to be sworn in by the bailiff."

The bailiff addressed Liz. "Please, raise your right hand. Do you swear to tell the truth, the whole truth, and nothing but the truth?"

When Liz said, "I do," Claire cringed. Whatever Liz was going to say would be a lie. She watched Liz walk to the witness stand. Dressed in a business suit and her hair pinned on top of her head into a bun, she looked smart and confident. She gave the jurors a smile and looked expectantly at the judge.

"Please, for the record, state you name."

"My name is Elisabeth Belmont." She smiled again. "Nobody calls me Elisabeth. To my friends I'm known as Liz. I am the widow of Andy Belmont. My husband was killed in a riding accident two years ago." Her face darkened and she pointed at Claire. "It was her fault."

Roy stood up and called, "Objection, your Honor. The witness's statement is not relevant to this case."

"Sustained. Missis Belmont, this trial is to establish the defendant's guilt in her husband's death, not your husband's."

240

"I'm sorry, your Honor. I thought it may be important."

To the prosecutor the judge said, "You may examine the witness."

"Thank you, your Honor. Missis Belmont, please tell the jury what you found the morning in question."

"I found the defendant lying unconscious on the floor. When I went to check up on her, I saw her holding a bloody knife. Looking around, I saw Allan, her husband, lying not far from her. I rushed over to him. He lay with his face down. There was blood all over the floor and then I saw the stab wounds in his back. There must have been more than a dozen. His head had been crushed. Seeing the frying pan beside him, I suspected it was the weapon used. I went back to the defendant and decided to take pictures. Then I called 911. The defendant woke up soon after that. When she saw me, she flung away the knife and said, "I didn't do it."

"Tell me, what prompted you to drive to your brother-in-law's house that morning?"

"Allan called me the day before and told me he was worried about Claire's state of mind. Apparently, she was making up stories, like being kidnapped and people wanting to kill her." She chuckled. "Would you believe, she even accused me of being behind the kidnapping she imagined. I cannot attest to this, but Allan said he found things in her bedroom that alarmed him. She had a copy of the Koran in her closet and clippings from magazines about terrorism and terrorist attacks. When he found a burka, he confronted her and she

241

told him it meant nothing. It was just some fantasy she had, and she kept wondering what it would be like to live in the desert and be the bride of a member of ISIS. Lately, she's been disappearing for days. He didn't know where she had been and what she was doing. She moved out a couple of weeks ago and had just come back. That's when she claimed to have been abducted."

Listening to her fantastic story, Claire couldn't control her anger and yelled, "It's true. I was abducted. You should know. You are telling lies, nothing but lies, you dumb bitch."

The judge threw her an annoyed look. "Councillor, please keep your client in line. One more outburst and I will hold her in contempt of court."

"I apologize, your Honor," Roy said, "it won't happen again." To Claire he said in a low voice, "Don't do that. You're not helping your case."

"I'm sorry, I couldn't help myself, but that bitch is lying through her teeth."

She wondered what kind of answer Liz would give when the prosecutor asked, "Missis Belmont, what was your relationship like with Claire before this? Did you get along? Did she ever display negative feelings toward you? Did you resent her in any way?"

"I always liked her. Not once did I imagine she would accuse me of something I'd never do to anyone. Who would have thought she was capable of murder? It goes to show we never know the people we associate with, not even our closest friends."

"Thank you, Missis Belmont. No further questions for this witness."

The prosecutor sat down and Roy stood up. "Missis Belmont, did you see any of the things Mister Belmont apparently found in his wife's bedroom?"

"Not personally, but I had no reason to doubt Allan. Why would he lie to me?"

"I wouldn't know." Roy addressed the judge. "Your honor, were any of those mentioned items presented as evidence?"

"Not to my knowledge. Please, proceed with questioning the witness, unless you're done."

"I'm not done. Missis Belmont, I understand that you pulled away from the rest of the family after your husband's death and never showed up on any family functions. When your husband died, did your husband's share of the company transfer to you?"

"Objection," called the prosecutor. "Not relevant."

"It is relevant, your Honor," Roy said. "I'm trying to establish the grounds for my next questions, as they will prove that Missis Elizabeth Belmont had no love for my client. She blamed my client for the death of Andy Belmont, her husband. In fact, she also hated her father-in-law, Aaron Belmont, and her brother-in-law, Allan Belmont. Allan would never confide in her and ask her to come to his place. You will understand my reasoning when Missis Belmont answers my question."

"There is something I don't understand, Councillor. Why did you object when Missis

Belmont accused the defendant of being responsible for her husband's death?"

"I didn't know which direction my examination of the witness's statements would take. I apologize, your Honor."

"I'll let it go this time. Please, answer the question, Missis Belmont."

"If you must know, I got nothing." Liz looked defiant at the judge and then at Roy. "Happy now?"

"Not really." Roy chuckled. "What prompted you to go to Allan's residence that morning?"

"I told you. Allan asked me to come."

"Okay, we'll leave it at that. Why did you call Detective Ron Salsky specifically to investigate the murder scene?"

"I didn't call him. I called 911."

"Actually, you didn't. You called the 23rd precinct and asked for Detective Ron Salsky. I checked it out, so don't bother denying it."

"Okay, I admit calling Ron Salsky. I had his number in my purse and I figured he would be there faster than if I called 911. He told me to call him in an emergency."

"How do you know Detective Salsky?"

"He was the one on the scene when my husband died."

"Do you not in fact have a relationship with Detective Salsky? One that started soon after your husband's accident?"

"I do not. Ron Salsky and I are friends, that's all."

"Did you orchestrate the kidnapping of Claire Belmont and are you behind the murder of her husband, Allan Belmont?"

A surprised moan went through the spectators when he asked that.

"Objection, your Honor," the prosecutor called in a loud voice. "Mister Sanders is baiting the witness with that preposterous question."

"Sustained. Councillor will refrain from speculating."

"No further questions at this time, your Honor." Roy sat down.

"Prosecution, you may call your next witness."

"The prosecution asks for a recess until our next witness arrives."

"When will that be?"

"Hopefully after lunch, your Honor."

The judge looked at his watch. "Alright. Court will recess until fourteen hours."

There was a restaurant across the street from the courthouse. Roy, Sylvia, and Claire went to have something to eat.

"I'm not really hungry." Claire looked at the menu without much enthusiasm. "Where did Liz get this crap about me being involved with Muslims? I've never seen a copy of the Koran and I have no desire to ever read one. My parents were religious, I never was. Why would I be interested in studying or even joining a religion like Islam, where women are treated like second class citizens? A religion that spawns groups like ISIS and other misguided radicals that terrorize the world by using their own people to blow themselves up and therefore murdering innocent people that never harmed them? That burka I wore when I came home was not mine. My abductors forced me to wear it. To wear

245

something like that is degrading. I'd never wear one willingly."

"Don't worry too much about that. When the time comes, we will make sure the jury hears your side. Let the prosecutor present his material. After that, we will present ours. Now, order something. Anything will be better than that prison food you've been eating."

Claire glanced at the guard sitting at the table next to them. "I'm glad he didn't insist on joining us. That would really have spoiled my appetite."

"Well, I'm going to order," Sylvia announced. "I'm hungry." She touched Roy's hand. "You looked great in there. I enjoyed watching you. I've never been to a court case. This is exciting."

"You wouldn't think so if your ass were in the hot seat," Claire said, sourly. She resented Sylvia for being there.

When they returned to the courtroom, she saw Salsky among the spectators. He pretended not to see her as she walked past him and she didn't acknowledge him, either.

He was the next witness for the prosecution.

"Please, state your name and occupation."

"My name is Ron Salsky. I'm a police detective with the 23rd precinct."

"Detective Salsky, you were the arresting officer on the scene. Please, tell the court and the jury what you found."

"I found the defendant, Missis Claire Belmont, standing in the kitchen of the Belmont residence, her clothing covered with blood. On the floor, not far from where she stood, lay her husband, Allan

Belmont, in a pool of blood. Missis Liz Belmont, the deceased's sister-in-law, was also present. Upon examination of the prone body of Mister Belmont, I saw more than a dozen stab wounds in his back. The back of his head looked crushed, evidence of one or more blows to his head. Then I saw the frying pan beside him, most likely the instrument used to inflict the crushing blows."

"Do you have a witness who can testify to that?"

"Yes, my partner Constable Langdon. He was the arresting officer. It's all in the police report."

"Thank you, Detective. No further questions."

Judge Milner looked at Roy. "The defence may cross-examine the witness."

"Thank you, your Honor." Roy left his place and walked closer to the witness stand. "Detective Salsky, have you and Claire Belmont ever met before the arrest?"

"Yes, we have, two years ago. I took her statement when her brother-in-law, Andy Belmont, died of a broken neck after he was thrown from his horse."

"After that?"

"I don't remember."

"You don't remember. Maybe I can refresh your memory. It was this year. Claire and her girlfriend, Carmen Garcia, witnessed you and a man by the name of Mohan Bakshi drown a man. His name was Joe Moretti."

"Objection. Councillor is accusing the witness of a crime that is pure speculation."

247

"Sustain." The judge gave Roy a stern look. "Mister Sanders. I'm warning you. You may not fabricate stories like that."

"They are not fabricated, your Honor. Detective Salsky has been investigated in that case. It's a matter of record."

"The case was dismissed in court, your Honor," Salsky announced loudly.

The judge banged his gavel onto his desk. "Detective Salsky. Please refrain from speaking when not instructed to do so. And you, Councillor, do not introduce cases that have already been dealt with in court."

"I withdraw my statement. May I continue to question the witness?"

"You may do so."

Ron turned back to Salsky. "Detective, are you in a relationship with Missis Liz Belmont? Please, answer carefully. We already spoke with Missis Belmont."

"We are friends. Sometimes I take her out for coffee."

"No romantic affair?"

Salsky turned to the judge. "Do I have to answer that, your Honor?"

"You don't have to. It is not relevant to the case."

"Thank you, your Honor." Turning back to Roy, he said with a little smirk on his face, "You heard the judge."

"I did, but that's okay. I'm satisfied with your answer. Your reaction to the question told me all I need to know. One more question. What is your connection to Mohan Bakshi?"

Salsky gave a casual shrug. "We're acquaintances. He's a lawyer. I hired him to represent me when I had to sue a car dealer. Other than that, we don't associate."

"That's it?"

"Pretty much."

Roy chuckled softly. "I hope you'll remember this answer, because I may ask you again as this trial progresses. No more questions for this witness, your Honor."

"You may step down, Detective Salsky. Defense, you may call your first witness."

"Thank you, your Honor. I call to the stand Randy Forrest."

Randy took his spot on the stand. After he introduced himself and was sworn in, he stood waiting to be cross-examined.

"Mister Forrest, how would you describe your relationship with Claire Belmont?"

"Claire and I are good friends. I've known her for a number of years. She keeps her horse at my ranch and she comes by often to ride her horse."

"Does she ever stay overnight at your ranch?"

"She does, whenever it gets too late to drive home."

"Where does she sleep?"

Claire began to wonder where Roy was going with his questions and began to feel uncomfortable. Her private life didn't have to be broadcast to all these people in the courtroom.

"I own a large house with many guestrooms. I have people staying at the ranch quite often."

"Did you have an incident at your ranch on the night of July 23?"

249

"Yes, we did. Two men drove into the yard and shot two of my horses. When I went to investigate what the shooting was all about, I was shot and wounded by one of the intruders. I defended myself and shot both men."

"You killed them?"

Randy nodded. "I did. It was self-defence."

"Objection," the prosecutor called out. "The witness is not on trial here."

"No, he isn't, but the event is connected to my client."

"Overrule. Let's hear it."

"Thank you, your Honor. Mister Forrest, who were the two men you shot?"

"They were known to the police. Both men had mob connections. The investigation is still ongoing, I cannot say more."

"What reason would they have had to shoot your horses? Did you ever have problems with the mob?"

"Not that I know of. Claire and I believe they were after Claire's horse, in retaliation for the beating I gave a Mohan Bakshi."

"Interesting. Why would you beat up this man? What did he do to you?"

"Not to me. To Claire. He blackmailed her demanding one million dollars from her for certain pictures he had. She lured him to a hotel room, promising to pay him. I went with her. When he tried to rape her, I came out of the closet I had been hiding in, and confronted him. He attacked me and things happened after that. I'm an ex-marine and capable of defending myself when attacked. I beat

250

him up. He deserved it. He's a slime-ball and also responsible for Claire's kidnapping."

"Objection. Witness is speculating."

"Sustained."

"That's okay. No further questions." Roy sat down and turned to Claire. "Don't worry. I had a good talk with Randy before I put him on the stand. He agreed to testify and only say things that are relevant."

"Thank you, Roy."

The trial was scheduled to continue after the weekend. Claire spent three nights in her cell worrying. Roy came by on Saturday and gave her a small stack of computer printouts.

"I took the liberty to write a postscript of the events that happened to you from the day you saw Salsky and Bakshi drown Joe Moretti. I left out all the private stuff that is not important to the case. Read it through and then sign it. I will hand this to the judge on Monday morning before the trial begins. I had a conversation with Detective Morgan and she agreed to testify on your behalf. She'll be there Monday. Apparently, they've discovered evidence that will support your story. She didn't give me any details."

Claire read everything carefully and signed it. "Do you think it will help?"

"I believe so. I would have put you on the stand, but you will never be able to recall all the important details you told me about. You'll be too nervous. Besides, the prosecutor would ask questions that would make you uncomfortable."

251

Claire looked at Roy with tears in her eyes. "Thank you for caring so much, Roy. You are the only one I trust with my life and I have faith in you. If anyone can get me out of here, it is you. I'm only sorry things worked out this way."

"That's life, Claire. Things have a way of happening, things we have little control over. I still care for you. That will never change."

The courtroom was packed when she entered it Monday morning. Roy smiled at her and said, "I handed everything to the judge, but we may not need it. There have been some interesting developments."

Claire just nodded, anxious to have the trial continue. She barely heard the bailiff and the judge as they opened the proceedings. When she saw Detective Morgan take the witness stand, she wondered if what she was going to present would be helpful in her case.

Roy approached the witness. "Detective Morgan, please tell the court how you became involved in the case of Missis Claire Belmont."

"I was the one who interviewed Missis Belmont when she was brought to my precinct after being involved in a car accident."

"How was she dressed?"

"She wore a burka. Apparently, the first thing she did was ask for a pair of scissors so she could cut off the part that covered her head."

"Does that sound like a woman who would willingly wear a burka?"

Morgan shrugged. "I didn't give it much thought."

252

"Tell the court what Missis Belmont told you."

"She told me she'd been kept prisoner in an old warehouse and that her kidnappers were on the way to the airport where a private plane would take her to Saudi Arabia."

"In other words it wasn't by her own free will to travel to Saudi Arabia?"

"That's what is sounded like."

"Did she tell you who she suspects to be behind her kidnapping?"

"Yes, she did. She said it was a man by the name of Mohan Bakshi and her sister-in-law, Liz Belmont."

"Why does she suspect them?"

"She witnessed Mohan Bakshi and another man drown a man. They knew she did observe them commit the crime and they warned her not to go the police."

"Who was the other man?"

"Ron Salsky."

"Detective Ron Salsky?"

"That's correct."

Roy looked around the courtroom and then focused on the jury. "Ladies and gentlemen of the jury, you heard. Please, make a note of that." He turned his attention back to Morgan. "How does her sister-in-law, Liz Belmont, fit into this?"

"Liz Belmont blames Claire for her husband's death."

"That is not something Claire Belmont made up. Liz Belmont already admitted to that herself. Let's jump forward now. What have you discovered that confirms Claire Belmont's claim to have been abducted and held in confinement?"

"What we've learned came to us purely by accident. A group of young people entered an old, abandoned warehouse in one of the industrial areas, looking for a place to party. They discovered a purse and a length of chain fastened to a radiator. When they rummaged through the purse, they found a driver's licence and other papers belonging to Claire Belmont. They dropped everything off at my precinct."

"Something else?"

"Yes. We found a phone belonging to Claire Belmont on one of the men that were in the car where she was a passenger."

"The car that crashed?"

"That's correct."

"Thank you, Detective Morgan." Again Roy made a show of scanning the courtroom. "Your Honor and ladies and gentlemen of the jury, this proves that my client, Claire Belmont, has been telling the truth." Turning back to the detective, he said, "How did you follow up on the evidence?"

"Since Missis Belmont's abductors had clearly been foreigners, we contacted the FBI."

Roy addressed the judge, "Your Honor, I have no further questions for this witness, but she mentioned the FBI, and it is most important to follow the thread. I would like to call to the stand Special Agent Bernie Heisinger."

"Objection." The prosecutor sounded agitated. "I have questions for this witness."

"Overrule," the judge said. "I will allow the next witness to testify. You can cross-examine both of them later." Then he said to Detective Morgan. "You may step down."

Claire watched with great interest as the FBI agent was sworn in. After taking the witness stand, Roy questioned him, "Special Agent Heisinger, what did you do after Detective Morgan contacted you?"

"The information we received from Detective Morgan only confirmed what we already knew. I cannot give you any details, but Kaito Tanaka and his company were already under investigation, as was his legal advisor Mohan Bakshi. Mister Bakshi has been arrested and charged with the murder of a Joe Moretti, among other offences. His accomplice, Detective Ron Salsky, is being arrested as we speak, charged with the same crime. Other charges against him are pending."

"Will they also be charged with kidnapping Missis Claire Belmont?"

"Not yet, but we are working on that as we gather more information."

Roy turned to Claire and gave her an encouraging smile, before addressing the FBI agent again. "As you are aware, my client is charged with the murder of her husband. She claims she didn't commit that murder. Can you provide any evidence that may help to prove my client's innocence?"

"Yes, I can. Mohan Bakshi gave us the names of the two men responsible for Allan Belmont's murder in exchange for immunity. Both men have been arrested."

Claire put her hands over her face when she heard those words. She became aware of a hush in the courtroom and then surprised shouts.

"Order in the court." The judge used his gavel to punctuate his words.

The shouting stopped.

Roy faced the spectators. His face was lit up with a big smile. "There is more," he said to the hushed crowd and turned back to the FBI agent. "Please, go on, Special Agent Heisinger."

The agent looked at the judge. "Your Honor, I have a sworn statement from Mohan Bakshi and a request for the arrest of a certain person in this courtroom. All I need is your signature."

Judge Milner frowned. "This is highly unusual. Mister Sinclair, please, bring the statement and request to me."

The bailiff took the envelope from the agent and carried it to the judge's desk. It was silent in the courtroom while the judge read the documents. After he was done, Judge Milner looked up, his face solemn. Then he spoke to the bailiff, "Mister Sinclair, please, arrest Missis Elizabeth Belmont for orchestrating the kidnapping of Missis Claire Belmont and the murder of her brother-in-law Allan Belmont."

Hearing those words, Claire broke down and cried, barely aware of the pandemonium in the courtroom.

After things quieted down a bit, Roy walked over to face the jury. "Ladies and gentlemen of the jury. After hearing the testimony of Detective Morgan and Special Agent Heisinger, you have no choice but to find my client, Missis Claire Belmont, not guilty."

Chapter Seventeen

Shivering a little, Claire pulled her sweater closer around herself. The evenings were getting cooler with every passing day. It was clear to see that fall was coming to an end.

"What are you thinking, girlfriend?"

She looked at Carmen, who didn't give the impression of being warm. "I'm thinking we should go inside and have a stiff drink to warm us up."

"I thought you'd never ask." Carmen got up, took her wine glass and emptied it. Then she followed Claire into the house. "Too bad we can't jump into the pool. I've always enjoyed going for a swim in the evening, but not in winter weather like this." She shook herself.

Laughing, Claire said, "Wait until it gets really cold. You may not want to leave the house at all."

"I've never been a winter-person. I don't know how those people up there in Canada survive."

"What brings that up?"

"I got an e-mail from a cousin who lives in Toronto. She invited me to come and visit her, but I don't even have the desire. I'd rather go south where it's warmer."

"Randy wants to go to the Mayan Riviera. He's been there a couple of times already. I've never been anywhere. Allan wasn't the kind of person to go on holidays."

Carmen walked over to the liqueur cabinet and pulled out a bottle. "Ah, tequila," she said. "This will warm us up."

257

"Not for me. I'd rather have something sweet, but not right now." She flopped down on the chesterfield. Looking around the room, she said, "I have to get rid of most of these statues. Allan bought them without ever asking me if I liked them. I didn't then and I still don't."

"Well, you can do what you want. The house and the property are yours now. You don't have to ask anyone for permission." Carmen poured herself a drink. After sitting down in one of the wide chairs, she mused, "Funny how things work out sometimes. A year ago, your future looked bleak. Allan threw you out of the house, you were blackmailed, then kidnapped, and then accused of Allan's murder. Now you own the house and everything else. You are a partner in the company and Randy wants to marry you. How much better can it get?"

"I don't know," Claire mused. "It all began when we witnessed the murder of a drug dealer. Who would have guessed that a horrible act like that would change my life forever? For the better, in many ways."

"Have you heard from Roy?"

"The last I heard he and Sylvia got married."

"Do you still love him?"

"I still have feelings for him," Claire admitted. "They will stay with me. Let's face it, we have history together, and my memories of him are happy memories. Destiny had other plans for both of us and I have to accept it."

"What about Randy? He seems to love you."

"He does. I love him, too. I believe his feelings for me are genuine, I know that, but I'm not sure if I want to marry again. At least not now. We'll see what the future brings."

Carmen gave her a thoughtful look. "I've been married three times and I'm happy with staying single. Perhaps, because I haven't found the right man, but men like Randy don't come along every day. As I told you before, he's a good man, and if I were in your shoes, I'd be worried he may get away. You're a rich woman now, and there are many men eager to make your acquaintance, eager to get into your bed, but most of them have ulterior motives. They don't want you; they want your money. Randy isn't one of them. He's the real deal. So, don't wait too long with your decision. Just saying."

"I know exactly what you're saying." Claire sighed. "Deep down, I know you're right, but I just don't know."

Carmen lifted her glass. "Here's to the good life and to the day when you know. Cheers."

THE END

About the Author

Herbert was born in Germany. Even as a young boy he was already a voracious reader. He read every book in the small School library at least three times. His teacher gave him even a few books from his own private collection. His favourite books were stories about heroes and gods. He loved the old legends. At age fourteen, a friend gave him a Science Fiction book and he fell in love with the story, wanting more. He saved his allowance to buy every SF book he could find; there weren't many, because Science Fiction was a new genre in Germany, but he also loved Westerns and Mysteries. When he turned seventeen, he became a member of the Science Fiction Club Deutschland (Germany), a club still in its infancy. He was thrilled to receive a passport with his picture in it, signed by Walter Ernsting, the president of the club. He was member number 735. He could never find enough SF stories to read, so he began writing his own. One of his short stories was made into a play and broadcast via radio to schools in Germany. In his early twenties, he immigrated to Canada. He began reading books written in English and studied to become proficient in this new language. And there was no better way to learn than to also write. Writing became his passion and he enjoyed making his fertile imagination come alive in his stories. During his lunch hour, he wrote into a scribbler and at home he pounded away on his manual typewriter whenever time allowed. The majority of his stories were Science Fiction. With the arrival of computers and the internet it suddenly became a lot easier to write, and, most importantly, to get published. His first full length novel 'Daughter of the Dark', Book one of his 'The Xandra' series was published in 2006 by Midnight Showcase. Then followed Book two 'Mother of Light' and Book three 'Goddess of Life'. The series has since grown to eight volumes. So far, Herbert has published more than 30 books in different genres. Most of Herbert's stories contain erotica and are for adult readers. To find out more about Herbert's books, please, visit his website and his blog.

Website: http://www.fictitioustales.weebly.com/
Blogs:
http://www.hegro.blogspot.com/
http://www.hergros.blogspot.com/

www.ingramcontent.com/pod-product-compliance
Lightning Source LLC
Chambersburg PA
CBHW010832250626
47157CB00010B/3260